Crack

Clancy. L.

By the same author

FIX

Crac

Leo

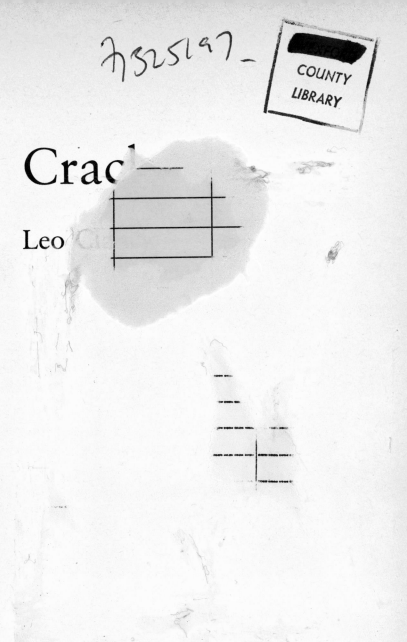

Secker & Warburg
London

First published in England 1986 by
Martin Secker & Warburg Limited
54 Poland Street, London W1V 3DF

Copyright © Leo Clancy 1986

British Library Cataloguing in Publication Data

Clancy, Leo
  Crack.
  I. Title
  823'.914[F]   PR6053.L28/

ISBN 0–436–09990–X

Printed and bound in Great Britain by
Biddles Ltd, Guildford and King's Lynn

For Gillian Wisher

Beasley, his face fevered in the red and yellow hues from the neon sign, touched Toaster with his elbow. "Someone's coming."

Toaster opened his eyes and crouched towards the windscreen. On the tarmac, between the van and the electric tic from the nightclub, a lamp-post stretched a shadow along the warehouse wall.

Beasley bent forward to lower the volume on the radio. "Is that him?"

"Who else is that big?"

"Weird. A bloody Highland ghost, the phantom bag-piper."

"I know what that is," said Toaster. "You stay put." He slid open the door and stepped onto the car park. He walked across to the wall and waited.

"That you, Toaster?" said Goff.

"Yeah."

"What are you skulking about like that for?"

"You never know. What the hell is that?"

Goff was carrying a plastic bag in his left hand, cradled to his chest. A tent-shaped piece of sacking protruded from the bag and rested against his shoulder. He dipped the bag towards the van. "That's a clever bit of parking. How do we get out if there's trouble?"

"There's a little alley at the back into a side street. That's where I've parked the spare motor. Let me see the gun, Tom."

Goff held up his right hand, palm forward. "Now look, Toaster. I don't want you to lay a finger on this weapon. You understand? Not a finger. It's cleaner than a Jewish kitchen and I don't want you pawing it up."

"What is it?"

"A Remington pump with an eight-shot magazine."

"A riot gun."

"That's what they call it. Stop 'em or start 'em."

"You've cut the barrel?"

"No. Eighteen inches. They make them like this over there. Now, let's get inside."

They entered the van. Toaster took the middle seat and Goff sat behind the driving wheel.

"Evening, Mr Goff," said Beasley.

"Hello, Graham. How have you been?" Goff turned and placed the carrier bag on the floor behind the seat. "I was just telling Toaster. I don't want either of you touching this."

"That's your musical instrument," Toaster said to Beasley. "Only plays the funeral march."

"Stay well clear of it, that's all," said Goff.

"Christ, Tom," said Toaster. "Don't make such a fuss. We're both wearing mittens." He held up his gloved hands.

"I noticed that and it's good," said Goff. "But let me tell you something." He jerked the thumb of his left hand towards the carrier bag. "When I went to collect that hoor, I elastoplasted each and every one of my fingers. Then I covered them in surgical gloves. Then I put the leathers on. And then I oiled the tips. Now, why do you think I went to all that trouble, Toaster?"

"We all know you're a careful man, Tom."

"Careful's not enough. You need a bit of respect for science. Those bastards can take a cigarette stub and tell you the last time you shagged your wife. When all this is over that gun'll be more dangerous than rabid beer. And if they ever do find it, I don't want them looking for any of us."

"They can't get prints from gloves, Tom."

"That's what you say, Toaster. But then I haven't seen your diploma in forensic medicine."

"Come on now."

"Look, Toaster, if and when they can lift prints from gloves, I suspect they won't be advertising the fact in the *Police Gazette*. So just leave it alone. Right?"

"I won't even look at it."

"Good," said Goff. He cleared moisture from the windscreen with the back of his glove. "That's the place, is it? God in tin. What does that say?"

"Good Intentions," said Toaster. "Some of the letters have gone to hell."

"Very good. Dry, but melting," said Goff. "You ought to be more serious when we're working, Toaster. Where's the entrance?"

"You can't see it from here. It's behind that brick extension, to the right of the sign. That's their motor, just beyond the lamp-post. The big Ford. The two Japanese jobs near the entrance, they were here last week and still there when we left. Probably staff. The Range Rover arrived after we rang you. They look like law as well. Three of them, all in civvies."

Goff spread his arms on the steering wheel and rested his chin on his hands. "You mean there's only seven punters in there? All law? Our four and the three from the Range Rover?"

"It's just a dive, Tom. Probably a drinking den run by an ex-copper. Maybe he's doing a bit of receiving on the side."

"The sergeant and Kilbride," said Goff. "There's no doubt about them?"

"They're there," said Toaster. He turned to Beasley. "And maybe one of the others?"

"I'm pretty sure it was Davis," said Beasley.

Goff sat up and stretched his shoulders. "Pity about the Inspector."

"He was at the pub," said Toaster. "Just like last week. Probably went home early to try on a new dress."

Goff kissed his teeth. "They have much to drink at the pub? Stay for afters?"

"No. Just late enough to antagonize the bar staff."

Goff grunted. "So," he said.

9

"I'm not worried about the Oaf, Tom," said Toaster. "You paid him well from all I've heard."

"How long did they stay last week?" said Goff.

"They left about two," said Toaster. "There was another couple of motors here by then."

"What state were they in?"

"Loud, but straight. Fairly straight."

"No merriment?"

"Not really. They just took off."

"All right," said Goff. "It looks good." He pushed open the sliding door and stepped out of the van. "I'm going to con the area. You two stay here. And, Toaster, leave the gun alone." He pulled the door shut.

Toaster moved across the seat to sit behind the steering wheel. He rubbed the side window and cupped his hands around his eyes. "That Tom," he said. "A great respect for science. He probably thinks a test tube's a new type of lager."

"He's in a right mood," said Beasley.

"That's just his style," said Toaster. "Edgy and cranky until the flag falls. Then he's as cool as a Royal smile."

"How would you know? I thought you said you'd never worked with him."

"That's true," said Toaster. "But I've worked with plenty who have."

"It all seems a bit casual to me," said Beasley. "He just strolls up with the world's biggest shooter and decides to have a look around. Meticulous planning, that's what I expected."

"Not when it's people, Graham. Banks and buildings don't look back. People do."

"I hope you're right," said Beasley, leaning forward to adjust the radio.

Toaster swung away from the window. "Leave that, Graham. How can you fuck about with Jim Reeves?"

"It's slop," said Beasley. "Blotting-paper slop."

"It's just what we need," said Toaster, correcting the dial. "Mood music. We're here for revenge, Beasley. We are the dark angels of the Lord."

10

"The victims of destiny."

"Victims? I don't like that, Graham. Do you remember what Tom said at the hospital when he was going over the alibi business?"

"No. When?"

"A couple of weeks ago. I don't know. He was doing the exercises and checking us out, giving us the third degree."

"Oh, yeah."

"Did you notice those weights he was lifting with his knees? The sweat was pouring off him and I thought, Christ, he's never going to get better. Then I checked out the weights myself. I couldn't lift them with my knees. And he was supposed to be the patient. I couldn't lift two-thirds that weight."

"So?"

"So I asked him. Why was he giving the old knees such a bad time when they were obviously so strong again. He said he wanted to be sure they'd forget they'd ever been victims. What about that, Beasley?"

"I think it's a crock," said Beasley, laughing.

"Oh, you do, do you?" said Toaster.

"Talking about alibis, Toaster," said Beasley. "Do you remember the one and only time we were partners in crime?"

"The tobacconist shop."

"Right. We were about sixteen or seventeen. And the coppers chased us and they caught you. I was hiding in a doorway, you know, and I could hear you yelling and screaming as they dragged you away. And next day me and Fred Wade went up to court and swore you couldn't have been anywhere near the shop because you'd been at a party with us?"

"And I was just running away because everybody ran from the Old Bill."

Beasley laughed again. "And one of the coppers grabbed hold of poor old Fred after he'd given evidence and accused him of being the one who got away."

They both laughed.

"It's funny," said Beasley. "I got away and stayed fairly straight ever afterwards. You got caught and went from bad to worse. There's a moral there somewhere."

"What do you mean, from bad to worse?" said Toaster. "I only dabbled now and then. I was doing really well with the videos until this nonsense."

"Bullshit," said Beasley. "If it wasn't for your seedy past, Kendellan, I'd have never got in touch with you about that cocaine business. And none of us would be here now. Victims of destiny is right."

"Nah," said Toaster. "I blame Sarah myself."

"Sarah?"

"Cherchez la femme, as Adam said. If she hadn't got me all upset that morning I'd never have drunk so much. And if I hadn't drunk so much, I'd never have been so stroppy in the pub. And me being stroppy is what really started them off. It's as plain as a plank of wood."

"Poor old Sarah."

"The only thing you've got right is the name, Beasley. Rich, young and lovely but very rarely serene."

"Poor old Sarah," said Beasley again.

Toaster linked both hands behind his neck and nodded towards the radio. "That's Sarah. A voice like a distant drum. The moment she opened her mouth that morning I knew a battle was coming. Far away, far, far away. I was washing my cock in the sink at the time."

"That couldn't have taken long."

"Ha, ha."

"What happened?"

Toaster took his hands from behind his head and traced his gloves around the steering wheel. "I don't want to talk about it." He turned up the volume of the radio with his left hand. "Listen to the music."

Toaster

He squeezed shampoo into the sink and coaxed the water into a froth with his fingers. His hips moved sideways and forwards on the edge of the basin.

"What are you doing?" she said, behind him.

His eyes flicked up at the mirror. She stood in the door-way, distraught through the sweating surface of the glass. Her dressing gown was secured at the waist with his neck-tie.

"I've got to wear that today."

"What are you doing?"

He raised his hands to his shoulders, spread his palms and wriggled his fingers. "Look, no hands."

"What is it?"

"Something disgusting, that's for sure."

"You're not peeing in the sink, are you?"

"Peeing is what little girls do." He dropped his hands into the water. "I dare say the song of a good slash is what woke you up."

She yawned. "You know I hate that word, Toaster."

"A poem in piss, then."

"Your arse is beginning to droop." She stepped up to the sink and rippled her hand through the water. "Look, it's catching."

He lifted her hand, shaking the wrist, strumming a spray of water. "I told you. I've got business."

She wiped her hand, front and back, on his chest. "So strong, so strong." She hitched up her dressing gown, sat on the lavatory seat and began to urinate.

"Charming," he said. "That's really charming, Sarah."

"Look who's talking. You'd rather use the sink when there's a loo two feet away."

"More hygienic," said Toaster. "No splashes on the seat, no puddles on the floor."

He took a towel from the rack and stepped away from the sink, drawing the towel up between his legs, shaking it open, wrapping it around his hips. He drew the plug upwards by its chain and turned on the cold tap, his fingers under the nozzle, spraying the basin walls.

"Time to taste the paste," he said. He pulled the mirror towards him and picked out his toothbrush and tooth-paste from the cabinet.

"My sister Marie was very particular about bathroom etiquette," said Sarah. "She used to go into a tantrum if she had to use the toilet after a man, even Dad, and the seat was left upright. She thought it was a sexual insult. An affirmation of superiority."

Toaster crouched into the sink, sawing away at the inside of his gums. "She was right."

"Sod it," said Sarah. "You've used all the bog paper. That's blissful, that is, really blissful."

Toaster spat into the sink and turned his head towards her. "Think dry."

"Give me the flannel. You were really brilliant last night."

"Was I? I thought you had a headache."

"Not that. You were wheedling. I can't stand wheedling."

"What's that mean? A word like that, so vague, it's bound to give offence."

"Never mind. I was talking about Sheila. You've got to be really brilliant to get Sheila off like that."

"She asked me, in that very sincere, precious tone of hers, she asked me not to call her sweetheart."

"Really? What did you say?"

"I'm afraid I became a little abusive."

"Toaster." Sarah stood up, shaking the gown loose from her thighs. She turned to flush the bowl. "Can't you ever behave?"

Toaster turned on the cold tap, cupped water from hand to mouth and tilted his head to gargle. Sarah ran her fingers through the flowing water and dried them on the towel around his waist.

"I mean, there must be lots and lots of people who don't want to be called sweetheart," she said.

"No doubt. Now cut that out, Sarah. Go and make a cup of tea."

"I'm going to watch you shave."

"Well, at least put the kettle on."

"Tell me about Sheila first."

"There's nothing to tell. I agree with you. There're probably plenty of reasons people don't like being called sweetheart. But voicing them? That's the stupidity. And that's what I told her."

"All kindness and grace, were we?"

"I said I was going past the dogs' home today and offered to look in on her relatives."

"You bastard. What did she say?"

"Nothing much. You know Sheila. Her bark's worse than her bite." He laughed and swayed towards her, kissing her on the mouth. "Kettle."

At the door, Sarah turned and said, "You're so funny. So, so funny."

Toaster arranged his shaving gear on the sink shelf. He fed hot water into the basin and bathed his face. He smeared his hand across the mirror and worked up a lather with brush and stick, dabbing the foam into the lower half of his face.

Sarah came back into the room carrying an ashtray and a lighted cigarette. She sat on the lavatory seat and placed the ashtray on the tiles. "Getting smooth and trim for Graham, are we?"

"What?"

"You told me last night. He was the only boy in school handsomer than you."

Toaster twirled the razor under the running tap. "Did I?"

"Don't you remember? You said you used to fancy him."

"Bullshit."

"Well, maybe you didn't. But everybody else did. Even the custard got hard. Your own words."

"He was a sweet youth," said Toaster. "But like all sweet youths he got acne." He swept the blade down the left side of his face, from the sideburns to the tip of the neck. "You have met him, you know."

"God, Toaster. We had this conversation in the taxi."

"Oh."

"I remember him quite well. He wasn't such a knock-out. His girl friend was, though. Clare something. Really stunning. Red hair, freckles and good teeth. Sable hat. Very nice."

"I thought you disapproved of furs."

"Well, I do. Because of the animals. But I've got to admit that people who wear them sometimes look so warm. You wanted to dance with her."

"Just being polite. I knew she wouldn't get much action out of Graham."

"Like that, is he?"

"Like what? What's wrong with you?"

"Shy."

"Shy? He couldn't look a cliff in the face. But that's not what you meant, Sarah."

"No?"

"No. You meant he didn't come when you put your hot little hand on his knee. So there must be something wrong with him."

"He wasn't very interested in her either, as I remember."

"Christ, Sarah, leave it out. She was all over him. Everything he did was divine. 'How divine, Graham. Oh, Graham, that's divine.'"

"Really?"

"He took it well, though. Threatened to turn her into a pillar of salt. He doesn't like dancing. He doesn't like attracting attention to himself. That's all I meant."

Sarah twisted her body off the seat to drop her cigarette into the bowl. "I thought he was mousy. He had freakish hearing, too. We played a game. Whispers or something."

Toaster tilted back his head and pulled the razor up over his chin.

"You're meeting him at the dog track, are you?" said Sarah.

"No. I'm meeting him in a pub."

"Then what was all that wit-of-the-week stuff last night about you going to the dogs?"

Toaster bent his nose to the left and stretched his top lip. He edged the razor around his nostrils. "I'm meeting Tom at the track. My uncle Tom. I don't think you know him."

"Is he the fascist?"

"No. That's Gerry. Tom's a real right-winger. He only believes in himself."

"What a swarm."

Toaster rinsed the razor and bent into the mirror, mouth open, bringing the blade down over his top lip. "Sarah, darling, you can't meet anyone today who's not some sort of fascist. Brotherly love can't get by in the technological age. The communications are too good."

Sarah stood, pushing the ashtray aside with her foot. "My, my, my. I think you must have swallowed some of that soap."

"Get the tea."

Sarah left, her wooden heels snapping against the tiles.

Toaster rinsed his face in cold water and turned off the taps. He dried his face and applied after-shave lotion, slapping his cheeks and running the back of his fingers along the bottom of his chin. He loosened the towel around his waist and let it drop to the floor. He wiped his feet on the towel and walked naked from the bathroom across the hallway and into the bedroom.

"Toaster," shouted Sarah.

"What?"

"No milk. Will you have it black?"

"No. Forget it."

Toaster threw his shirt and underpants onto the bed and sat down beside them. He took his socks from inside his shoes, sniffed at them and put them on. Sarah came into the room cradling a cup of tea without a handle, a cigarette alight in her mouth.

"You'll be declared a pollution zone," said Toaster.

"Please," she said. She placed the cup on the dressing table and sat in front of it, her left arm hanging over the back of the chair. "If only you were kinder, a little more loving, Toaster."

Toaster pulled his underpants up over his hips without getting off the bed. "Love. Kindness. That's for nuns. What we've got is love's big sister, lust."

"Lust is big and strong and frightens people," said Sarah, dropping her voice an octave.

"You do listen, then."

"Love is for papheads," said Sarah, in the same voice. "They want rules and rights and democracy and bogey men. And pap to keep it all together. And their patron saint is Humpty Dumpty."

Toaster picked up his shirt and ran his thumbs along the inside of the collar. "You got the lines a little tangled there, Sarah."

"What's that matter? It's all the same. And your friends. Glib. A good line in cynical waffle."

"And fuck you, too."

"One of the things I've always liked about you, Toaster, is that you're not foul-mouthed."

"Well, knock it off, then."

"You all work so hard at being articulate. But it never sounds quite right. Always a bit forced."

"Contrived is the word you're looking for."

Toaster sat upright on the edge of the bed and pulled the shirt over his head, shuffling his hands past the fastened cuffs. "Sarah, darling, have you ever thought how important it is, when you're talking, just how many people are listening? How what you say is given more weight by the number of ears in attendance. Bores don't travel in pairs, do they?"

"Sounds like more waffle."

"Probably."

Toaster crossed to the closet and took down his suit.

He slipped the trousers from the hanger and dropped the jacket and waistcoat on the bed. He examined the crease in his trousers. "Tom's got a mate called Con. Now, when it comes to the crack, Con's strictly second division. But he's got a great gimmick. He's worse than those TV politicians. He nearly always starts a sentence with an 'and'. You know what I mean? An 'and'. That way it seems he's always entitled to the floor because he's never quite finished. Tom says Con's always got three 'ands' up his sleeve."

Toaster laughed and stepped into the trousers, smoothing his shirt inside the waistband and zipping up his fly. "You get it?"

"Blissful," said Sarah. She lit a fresh cigarette from the old one and crushed the stub in the ashtray on the dressing table. "This Tom. He's the gangster is he? The mystery man Margaret's always on about. The one who had to go abroad?"

Toaster stood in front of her. "Your hair looks good, Sarah. Like blackcurrant jam." He noticed his neck-tie. "I need that," he said, kneeling to take it from around her waist.

"Well?" she said.

Toaster smoothed the tie back and forth between his fingers. "He's a highly respected businessman, Sarah. He didn't have to go abroad. A personal sacrifice on behalf of our balance of payments. The man's a patriot."

"An Englishman?"

"I don't think he could be accused of that."

"Who is he being patriotic for, then?"

"For Europe, Sarah. He's one of the new breed."

"And where did he have to go abroad to? Sicily?"

"Oh, you're so sharp. He's been to Canada actually. Travelling on his own passport, spending his own money, accompanied by his wife and three children. All right?"

Sarah balanced her cigarette on the ashtray and stooped in towards the mirror, both elbows on the dressing table, fluffing her hair. "What's he like?"

"Big. Bigger than me. Taller. About six-three. And

broader, too. A health freak. Tom was a health freak before butter got a bad name."

"I didn't mean that," she said.

Toaster crossed behind her, lowering his head into her hair, his mouth touching her ear. "He's cool and rich and hard."

Sarah pushed his head away with her right hand. "Stop it."

Toaster straightened. "He's like a big, mischievous kid. Loves laughing, does Tom. Everybody wants to talk to him, buy him a drink. He's got thousands, thousands. But that's not why. He's like a kerosene lamp in the jungle. He's irresistible. Tom's got power."

"What power?"

"I don't know. Just power. Power to attract, power to influence. He knows people."

"A villain," said Sarah.

"Christ." Toaster walked across to the mirror above the fireplace and fitted his tie under the collar of his shirt.

"What's the so-called business, then?" said Sarah.

Toaster looked at her over his shoulder. "You're in a right mood this morning."

"I'm frustrated. What's the business?"

"Tom's business?"

"No. With you and him and Graham."

"It's not really business. Graham wants an introduction. He's got information to sell and Tom's got contacts who might want to buy. I'm just the middle man. Any more questions?"

Sarah turned from the mirror, balancing her head on her left hand, squinting through the smoke. "Yes, here's another question. Why do men putting on a tie always stop and pose right in the middle of it, just like you're doing now. When they're going to say something, I mean. It can't be impossible to talk and tie at the same time."

Toaster, one end of the tie in each hand, slid it up and down and smiled at her. "I don't know. You're talking about films. I'm just a copycat."

"It's not just films."

22

Toaster tossed the tie into a knot and smoothed down the collar of his shirt. "I'll think about nothing else all day, Sarah darling. I suspect you've unearthed one of the last great secrets of the human psyche."

He swung back to the mirror, closing in on it, dabbing at his hair. "Do you think I'm vain?" he said to her reflection.

Sarah covered her mouth with her bottom lip and squeezed her chin. "You think you were left on a doorstep, don't you, Toaster?"

He looked up at her. "In a basket with a royal crest."

Her shoulders shuddered. She sat upright, flicking at the corners of her eyes with her thumbs. "I'm sorry. The dreaded giggles."

Toaster sat on the bed and began to put on his shoes.

"Were you ever in the Boy Scouts, Toaster?"

"This'll be even funnier, will it?"

"I'm serious."

"All right. I was never in the Boy Scouts. Why do you ask?"

"Don't be snotty. It's just that you reminded me of my kid brother there. Tying the laces like that. So exact. He had a funny hat and a long stick."

Toaster stood up, taking his waistcoat off his lap, tapping his feet on the carpet. "Have you been hitting the booze already?"

Sarah said, "You bastard." She swivelled towards the mirror, reaching for her cigarettes.

"Well? Have you?"

"You're just being a brute because I laughed at you."

"Is that what it is?"

Sarah lit a cigarette. "You've got spite seeping out of your eyes sometimes, Toaster. You'll say anything to wound. Anything. You have to hurt, don't you? Sometimes I think you're little more than a nasty creep. A melt, as some of your friends would say. A right melt."

"And you're sick of it."

"Well, I am. Sick of it all, the clever talk, the right way to behave. Everything's so personal with you, isn't it?

With all of you. A bunch of big babies. If you don't get your own way, it's mope, sulk and start a fight. If you have a bad day at work, if you can't get a taxi, if your horse loses, everybody has to pay. You complain about the beer in the pub. Or, if we go to the pictures, it's an awful film and everybody's rustling their sweet-papers. And, worst of all, a restaurant. We always get a bad table, the food's not fit for pigs and the service is a joke."

Toaster buttoned his waistcoat and looked over his shoulder into the mirror. "But you've got to admit I always leave a good tip."

"Yes, I have noticed that. But I don't think it does you much credit. Solidarity of the serving classes."

Toaster whirled to face her, clicked his heels together and bowed. He picked up his jacket from the bed and shook it by the neck. "I just worry about you, Sarah."

"No you don't, Toaster. You don't worry. You watch. Your only worry is that I might say something or do something that might embarrass you. It's yourself you worry about. You want everything under control. No emotional excess, please. Not while Mr Kendellan is part of the company. You're like a bloody school matron, Toaster. A killjoy. You're just like your damn laces."

Toaster laughed. "A killjoy."

"That's right. Thanks to you I get no joy out of men anymore. Oh, I don't mean that. I mean men generally. I used to become incandescent in the company of men."

"Incandescent."

"Yes, Toaster, incandescent. I used to glow. But not any more. Now I'm frightened that Toaster's watching with that bleak looking-at-something-else face. And that's when I need a drink."

Toaster put on the jacket and tapped the breast pocket. "Clean hankie?"

Sarah opened the bottom drawer of the dressing table and handed him a handkerchief. "What were you going to say?"

Toaster twisted the handkerchief into his top pocket. "It doesn't matter."

"Come on. It's probably so nasty you'll burn your mouth unless you get it out."

"It wasn't all that long ago, Sarah, that you told me you drank because you were frightened. Frightened of getting old, of being lonely, of having people put up with you. I was just wondering if drinking on my account is any improvement on all that."

"What a swine you are."

"That's better," said Toaster. He moved towards her. "Let's kiss and make up."

She turned her head away. "No. You'll only complain about my nicotine breath."

Toaster stood next to her chair. "This is bad timing, I know, Sarah. But I'm short again. Is it okay if I borrow a few quid?"

"Oh, God."

Toaster pulled out the middle drawer of the dressing table and took two notes from a leather wallet. He showed her the notes and placed them in his inside pocket. He kissed the top of her head and said, "Thanks, love."

Toaster collected his overcoat from the closet and walked towards the bedroom door.

Sarah stood up. "Just a minute, Toaster."

"What?"

She crossed to the side of the bed, picked up her handbag and carried it back to the dressing table. She turned to him, her head high, her voice raised. "Where's this bank of yours that's always so bloody inconvenient to get to?"

"Don't start."

"Where is it?"

"Cover yourself up, Sarah."

"Where is it?"

"You know where it is. Rickmansworth."

She opened her bag, took out her purse and tipped all the loose change onto the glass top of the dressing table. "Well then, when you've finished your business today, here's the bus fare to Rickmansworth."

Toaster folded his overcoat across his left arm and opened the bedroom door.

"Bus not good enough for you?" said Sarah. "Very well then." She took a handful of notes from the purse and threw them on top of the coins. "Here. Take a taxi. But for God's sake, stop poncing off me."

"Cool down, woman," he said.

She plunged her hand into the ashtray, closed her fist, slapped it down on top of the money and spread her fingers.

"And here's some cigarettes for the journey," she said.

She lifted her hand. The ash puffed into a cloud and two twisted butts uncoiled and rolled onto the carpet.

"You know I don't smoke," he said.

Sarah looked at her palm and wiped it against her dressing gown. She sat, turning away her face, her left hand covering her eyes.

"Sarah," he said.

"Just go," she said, extending her right hand and flicking the bottom of her fingers towards him. "Just go." The ash had edged between the joints and smeared her vermilion nail varnish.

The door closed.

"A right melt," she said.

Toaster came through the tunnel opposite the starting line. A bell rang and he stopped. The rail in front of him began to vibrate. The dogs whined and scratched in their boxes.

To his right were a line of bookmakers, still taking bets. At the far end of the stadium, high above them, a huge electronic totalizator board dazzled the changing odds.

Toaster began to climb the terracing. He stopped again as the mechanical hare whirred across the restraining bar and released the traps. The dogs broke, lunging forward and accelerating into the roar of the crowd.

Toaster was eased aside by a bald man wearing a red scarf high up around his ears. He turned to watch the race.

The bald man broke into a shouted prayer as the dogs skittered into the first bend. "Come on the six. Well away six. Get on boy. Go six, go six, go six."

Below Toaster, a man in a leather overcoat, a line of dribble running from his mouth, was screaming, "Go on one. Catch him, one. Catch him, one. Catch him, one."

The bald man raised his right arm, punching the air, "Six, six, six." A vein swelled in his temple.

The dogs swept around the final bend, chasing the six to the winning post. "You beauty, you beauty, you beauty," crooned the bald man.

The terraces began to thin as the loudspeaker announced the finishing order. Toaster stayed to watch the dogs. Across the patches of snow that lay dying in the middle of the stadium he could see the handlers on the back straight waving their leashes, throwing scraps of meat.

A hand gripped his elbow and Goff said, "Did you have the winner?"

Toaster spun around and shook hands, his face breaking into dimples. "Tom. Jeeze, it's good to see you. How are you? You're looking great."

"Aren't we all Toaster? Aren't we all."

"Christ, this place is fantastic. I'd no idea. Fantastic."

Goff, grinning, said, "What are you on about?"

Toaster swept out both arms and turned in a semi-circle. "The whole bloody scene. I'm astounded. I came in down there where they start and I was admiring the bookie's umbrellas and all the colours and I got the shock of my life when those boxes opened up. I could hear the sods but I didn't know where they were. And the people, Tom. Loony Tunes. Straight out of Loony Tunes. They're all dippy, Tom. They say everything in threes and think the dogs know what numbers they're wearing. There was a bloke here, you wouldn't believe it. He was betting a sore throat against a heart attack. Christ, it's good to see you. Tom. Where's Jacko?"

Goff hit him, open-palmed, on the shoulder. "In the bar. It was him who spotted you. Come on."

Toaster followed Goff's heavy blue overcoat up the terracing and through the glass doors into the lounge. Jacko was sitting at a table adjoining a pillar. His programme was held close to his eyes and he was holding his glasses in his left hand. Two empty chairs were tilted into the table.

"Hello, Jacko. Fair while," said Toaster.

Jacko placed the programme on the table and put on his glasses before shaking hands. "Sit down, son. Are you well?"

"Fit enough for the Olympics."

Jacko pushed the two tilted chairs back on their legs and looked at Goff, "High jump, probably."

Goff and Toaster sat down.

"Are all these ours?" said Goff, nodding at six bottles

of beer on the table. Three of the bottles had upturned glasses hatted over the tops.

"They are," said Jacko. "I had to kick sixteen Pakis out of here to get the table back. You didn't want something stronger, Toaster?"

"Christ, no," said Toaster. "I've had no breakfast." He looked at his watch. "It's hardly midday."

"That's the trouble with these morning meetings," said Jacko. "You tend to sleep the afternoon away." He half rose to lean across the table. He rubbed Toaster's earring between his thumb and forefinger. "I thought you had a growth or something."

"Don't worry about it, Jacko. It just means I'm bent."

"It means you're out of fashion. Your hair's too long as well."

Toaster smiled. "Vanity'll never go out of fashion."

"Stop teasing the lad," said Goff. He poured beer into a glass and handed it to Toaster. "So, how have you been?"

"I'm doing well, Tom. I expect the Inland Revenue to send me a Christmas card."

Goff laughed and squeezed Toaster's thigh.

"Jesus, Tom," said Toaster.

"It's good to see you. Doesn't he look well, Jacko?"

"A symbol of envy."

"How's your mother?" said Goff.

"You heard she moved into the country with Peggy?"

"I did. But how's she doing?"

"Crushing the seasons, Tom. Beating the earth into submission. Growing lettuces in January and God help the frost."

"Just so," said Goff, rocking back on the chair and puffing out his cheeks in a glitter of gold teeth. "And Paddy? Still out with the heathens?"

"Muslims, Tom, Muslims. An ancient and respected culture."

"Dickheads," said Jacko. "They fuck donkeys."

"Well," said Toaster, turning his palms upwards, "whatever they do, Paddy's teaching them to stop it."

29

Goff crouched towards the table, elbows on his thighs, cocking his head to one side. "So you're all alone in the big city now, Toaster?"

"As far as the family goes," said Toaster. He looked from one to the other. "What's the malicious smile for?"

Jacko raised his eyebrows to Goff.

Goff laughed. "We heard you'd got yourself a little sugar. Beauty, brains and a bank balance."

"Ray Lannigan's been broadcasting, has he?" said Toaster. "Radio Lannigan."

"It's true then?"

"A right little darling, Tom. What a combination we make. I've got the looks, she's got the loot. And she does my laundry, too."

"God, she's fearless."

Toaster raised his glass. "No. She's a good girl. A handsome woman. Incandescent in the company of men. You'll have to meet her. She pulled a stroke on me this morning that, well, it left me speechless."

"We're all ears," said Jacko.

"I'll bet. Speechless, I said. I couldn't tell it to a priest. Mind, now, I may well have deserved it. She said I was brutish."

"Brutish," said Goff. "I thought the English women were fond of that."

"They've got very little choice in the matter," said Jacko. He tilted his chin at Toaster. "How long have you been seeing this one?"

"Two years," said Toaster. "More."

"That long?"

"I'm a constant man, Jacko."

Jacko smiled at Goff. "Is he telling us he's a permanent shit?" he said, standing up, clipping his pen away inside his overcoat.

"I thought this one wasn't worth a bet," said Goff.

"It's not. But it might be worth a look. I'll see you in a minute, Toaster."

Goff turned his chair to watch Jacko pass through the swing doors.

30

"A sinful waste to be sitting here, Tom," said Toaster.

"Relax, there's plenty other races. These are just puppies. What do you think of Jacko?"

"Well, I could say he still looks bloody menacing."

"Why, doesn't he?"

"He's older, his hair's whiter, you could ski on those eyebrows."

"He still drives well."

"He walks like a man with something to hide."

"How's that?"

"Like he's being delicate with himself. He's not ill, is he?"

Goff shrugged, his face soured. "You're a great man with the balm, Toaster." He stood up. "Come on then, if you're so keen."

As they passed the Tote windows, Goff said, "There was never a better man than Jacko with the Glasgow Kiss."

"The what?"

Goff made a butting motion with his head.

"Oh," said Toaster.

"Now he forgets things," said Goff.

"Yeah? I'm told that's the definition of a good historian."

"Or a good wife."

On the terracing Toaster looked around and said, "There seems to be no great gathering of the superior classes, Tom."

"No. It's too serious for their women. There's no dog lovers here. They're all gamblers. Carpet wholesalers. Hamburger franchises. No glamour. No ethics. Some of the trainers throw a live rabbit into the kennel the night before a race."

"The hounds."

The crowd, hushed by the bell, swelled with noise as the hare snapped the boxes open. The two dog, wearing a blue jacket, took a clear lead at the first bend and was never troubled to the winning post.

"Look at these loonies," said Toaster, nudging Goff with his elbow. "I can't get over it."

"They lack your self-awareness, Toaster," said Goff, writing in his programme. "Can you see Jacko?"

"No. How was Canada, Tom?"

"Slow. Marion and the kids were stuck on the place."

"They're still there, aren't they?"

"They'll not budge, she says."

"And what about you?"

"I'll not go back. It was like living in a kitchen, Toaster. Either the fridge or the oven. And the central heating gave me a headache."

"You're not separating?"

"I don't know what else you'd call four thousand miles. She'll be all right. I've left her a couple of car parks. Steady income. She won't be short. And the kids aren't kids anymore."

"I thought you were going to become a citizen."

"That was the plan. Those immigration people. A hard bunch. They want to know your inside-leg measurement."

"What'll you do here, then?"

"I'm working on something. Give me a couple of weeks. We'll have a decent dinner. Bring your lady bountiful. Come on. He's probably back at the table."

The entrance to the lounge was blocked by two boys sorting through the discarded tote tickets.

"Give way," said Goff, stepping over them. He turned back to Toaster. "And how's the video game?"

"Oh, I'm coining it, Tom. Making a bomb on Asian epics. Won't last, though. Too many cowboys and not enough Indians."

Jacko was sitting at the table cleaning his glasses with a red silk handkerchief, "What a bunch of cowards," he said. "Did you see them bottle out at the first bend?"

"The winner could have stopped for a piss," said Goff.

"Odds on, I'm glad we left it alone."

"There's no better gift, Jacko," said Goff, looking at Toaster. "Knowing when to leave something alone."

"What does that mean?" said Toaster.

"Do you know who I saw out there, Thomas?" said Jacko, tapping Goff on the forearm. "As God is my judge, it was old Ironclad."

"Go on," said Goff.

"True. You'll see him yourself. Sniffing down there amongst the bookies, waiting for someone to drop a ticket. Wearing a flasher's mac and looking ninety in the shade. And them stepping around him like he's a pool of vomit."

"It's a wonder they let him in at all," said Goff.

"Who is he?" said Toaster.

"Oh, history, Toaster, history. We're talking about history," said Jacko. He topped up all three glasses from the last bottle of ale. "It must be, what, fifteen years, Tom, since he was at it?"

"More, I'd say," said Goff. "Twenty."

"Yeah?" said Toaster. "And what was his pitch?"

"A lovely, simple stroke," said Jacko. He swallowed beer and dabbed his handkerchief to his mouth. "He was a terror, Toaster, a terror. He'd collar some unsuspecting greenhorn like yourself in one of the tunnels downstairs. And remember, we're talking about a few years ago. Twenty, thirty thousand was nothing at those meetings. And, well, he'd pull you in tunnel sixteen, say, and tell you, 'I've got an ironclad winner here, lad. Don't give me any money. Not a penny. I'm not a con man. Just put a nice few quid on the three dog. You'll see. Meet me back here, tunnel sixteen, before the next race and I'll give you that winner, too. Remember now. The three dog. It's ironclad.' "

Jacko laughed and took another drink. "The cheeky monkey. Because of course, if the three dog did win, you'd be back there forcing a little drink on the reluctant old sod."

"I don't get it," said Toaster.

Jacko clapped his hands and held them open, palms upwards. "For God Almighty's sake, Toaster, can't you see? The crafty old boot has had six different punters in six different tunnels, each with a different dog. As long as he could remember which tunnel was which, he couldn't lose."

"Yeah, yeah," said Toaster. "Sure. Pretty good. But a lot of work. Every race, six tunnels. Isn't there an easier way, Jacko? Something a bit more subtle?"

Jacko turned to Goff. "Subtle, he says subtle."

"Did I say subtle?" said Toaster.

"Look, kid," said Jacko, "by the usual standards Ironclad was a ringer for that Nicky MacIvaley. The rest of them would as soon pitch a cat into the last bend if the wrong dog was winning."

"And those Cork bastards would leave the cat in a bag," said Goff.

"And those Kerry louts would probably blindfold the poor creature," said Jacko.

"And those scallywags from Limerick would tie its back legs together," said Goff.

"And still put it in a bag," said Jacko, laughing and rocking the table.

"Easy, now, easy," said Goff, smiling at Jacko's laughter.

"Have you seen that, Jacko?" said Toaster. "Losers stop a race, I mean."

Jacko pushed the tip of his handkerchief under his glasses and into the corner of his eye. "No. You, Tom?"

Goff shook his head.

"It must be a brutal sight," said Jacko. "Those dogs are going at a fair lick and anything they hit'll feel it. I saw a dog at Brighton one day. He was bumped at the first bend and just lay there, twitching and whimpering. The others ran on. And the kennel boy, maybe it was a bit of a pet, he hops onto the track and tries to pick the dog up in his arms. But the beast was skittery, heaving and squirming. It took the lad a long while to get the dog in his arms. And by the time he'd got it up and was staggering off the track, the pack had come round again. The leading dog hit the boy like that −" smacking his fist into his hand "− and it made your balls clench to see it. The dog died on impact. You could hear the crack of that lad's bone, high up here on the thigh, you could hear the

34

echo round the stadium like a rifle shot. And, do you know, the punters went wild. No sympathy at all. They were raging. They'd have gladly broken the other thigh. It was almost a riot."

"What were they upset about?" said Toaster.

"Well, it was a distance race, you see, and every last man of them convinced his money was on the winner."

"And there wasn't a winner?"

"Oh, no, not when it's as bad as that. They call the race void. Everybody gets their money back. Nobody likes that much. Not the organizers. And certainly not the bookies."

Goff tapped a finger on his programme. "Talking about the bookies. It's the four dog this next race, Jacko?"

Jacko nudged his glasses up over his brows and knuckled his eyes. "Only two or three dogs are ever entitled to win these races," he said to Toaster. "But only God and the trainers know what's going on."

"You mean dope and all that?" said Toaster.

"Oh, you don't need dope to stop the bastards. A pail of water'll do nicely. What are you laughing at?"

"A pail of water. The last time I heard that was in a nursery rhyme."

Jacko looked at Goff. "I thought you said he'd matured?"

"You did say the four dog?"

Jacko picked up his programme, pushed his chair back and stood. "That's right. Kitty's Dream. I'll check first, though. If the word's still good, what'll you have?"

"I'll chance a couple," said Goff.

"Toaster?"

"Not for me, Jacko."

"All right. I'll see you in a minute," said Jacko.

Goff placed his elbows on the table, bringing his hands up to form a funnel around his mouth, stroking his nose with the index fingers. "This should be a good gamble, Toaster."

Toaster shook his head. "Not my scene. Why does he get out so early?"

"He likes to hunt out the best odds. He enjoys scaring the shit out of the smaller bookies with a fistful of fifties." Goff closed his eyes and dropped his chin into the heels of his palms. "That other business doesn't look so good."

"No?"

"Well."

"He's turned it down, has he?"

Goff sucked a kiss against his teeth. "It's not like that."

"What do you mean?"

"It's never got that far. Yes, Jim'd have to say okay in the end. Everybody would. But I haven't even put it to him. You understand?"

Toaster moved his chair closer to the table. "Not really, no."

Goff picked up his glass and sent the liquid swirling up the sides. "You're going into one of your acts, Toaster."

"Am I? Which one?"

"Affronted innocence demands justice."

"Leave it out, Tom." Toaster undid the top two buttons of his overcoat. "Look. It sounded all right to you, didn't it? You had no objections yourself. I know everybody's got to say all right, okay. But if Tom Goff doesn't say all right, okay, then nobody says all right, okay."

Goff placed the beer glass on the side of the table and hunched forward. "So, you don't understand. It's not like you think anymore, Toaster. I've been away three years and back less than a month. That's point one. Point two and more important is that I've retired. I just don't do that nonsense anymore. It's dangerous, full of stress, bad for the heart. Sure, I meddle a bit, advise, maybe. But that still leaves me lame. I've got no clout. Now, what you told me, that sounded good, the sort of thing Jim likes. He loves the planning, the scheming, working out the edge. So I thought this might appeal to him. And, after all, you're Murty's son and I'm fond of you. The least I can do is look at what you tell me."

Goff turned his head towards the bar.

"All right, all right," said Toaster. "And what did you see?"

"Problems. It's not as good as you think, Toaster. It's not good enough to mention to Ralph, never mind Jim. It's got holes in it. It's not quite the way the waiter told you. It's not quite there at all, you see. So, what should I do? Put it up anyway so they can all say, 'Look at poor old Fu Goff. Lost his touch. He'll be bingo-bashing next.' Come on now, Toaster."

"Who's this Fu Goff?"

Goff tapped an index finger against his breast bone. "That's what they used to call me before I was big enough to dislike it. Say it again, quickly. Right, you've got it. They only use it now to needle me."

Toaster stretched back in the chair and cupped his hands behind his neck. "Graham lied then, did he?"

"Graham's the waiter?"

"Graham Beasley."

"Well, Toaster, I didn't say he lied. I said it's not quite the way he told it. That might not be down to him at all."

"The bastard."

"Aren't we all?"

Toaster swayed back into the table and put his hand on Goff's sleeve. "You've been wasting your time then, Tom?"

"A man who's doing a favour for a friend is never wasting his time."

"You're a good old stick, Tom Goff. What'll I do about Graham?"

"I thought you'd arranged a meet. I half expected to see him with you this morning."

"I wanted to say hello first. I said we'd be in the Castle around two and stay till closing time."

"That's good," said Goff. "We'll stick to that. It'll do no harm and you'll see yourself there's nothing else for it."

"You know the Castle?"

"Dean Street?"

"That's the one."

"Where the gents is always overflowing?"

"I don't know about that."

Goff moved his chair back and tugged his cuffs down. "Maybe it's improved then. It's been a long while. I once saw a young fellow in the Castle throw up into his glass and then swallow the vomit in the hope that no one would notice."

"Jesus, Tom."

Goff laughed and stood. "Certainly a miraculous performance, Toaster. But I'm sure it wasn't him. Come on, let's go dream about Kitty."

They watched the race from the strip of terracing in front of the glass doors.

"Reminds me of the sanctus, the way they all hush when the bell goes," said Toaster. "Waiting for the sacrament."

"I'd say you haven't been to mass for a while. It's not the sanctus anymore. It's all in English now. The vernacular, they call it. Like talking to God out of the corner of your mouth."

A man in front of them turned around to look at Goff. Goff smiled at him and tilted his chin towards the track. The man looked away.

"You still go, Tom?" said Toaster.

"I take the kids and savour the incense. I don't –" His words were smothered as the hare passed the traps and unleashed the dogs. "Oh, look at that four. Look at him go."

The four dog shouldered into the lead coming out of the first bend, switched inside and stayed close to the rail for the rest of the race.

"No danger," said Toaster.

"That'll please Jacko," said Goff. "Go and save the table while I get another round."

Jacko was already at the table when Toaster returned. He was smiling. "Did you see that little darling fly out of the trap? She must have had a hot coal up her arse. Where's himself?"

38

"Getting the champagne. Well done, Jacko."

Toaster sat down and Jacko rolled a cigar across the table to him.

"There," said Jacko. "Puff to my success."

"Please, Jacko. They give me a headache."

"Save it for someone else then."

Jacko removed the cellophane from his own cigar and spiked the end. "You had a chat with Tom all right? And he told you the bad news?"

"Yeah."

Jacko struck a match and held it beneath the cigar, away from his mouth, turning the cigar between his fingers. "Come on now, kid. Are you not a teeny bit relieved? It's not really your game, is it?"

"I'm only making the introduction."

"Oh."

"You didn't think I wanted to get on the team, did you, Jacko?"

Jacko placed the cigar in his mouth and drew a series of short puffs. "Well, maybe I did."

"Does Tom think that?"

"I wouldn't know about that. You know Tom. He thinks quiet."

Toaster pulled aside the top of his overcoat and dropped the cigar into the breast pocket of his jacket. "I don't need any of that. I was just doing a favour for someone. I'm happy with the videos."

"A favour for the waiter?"

"That's right. You know him?"

Jacko shook his head. "I know the nosh shop. Table linen's cleaner than the grub."

"And the bill's heavier than the Yorkshire pudding. No, seriously, it's in all the books."

Jacko balanced his cigar in the groove of the ashtray, took out his handkerchief and began to clean his glasses. "So, you're not into any villainy, Toaster? Didn't I hear something about Sainsbury's?"

"For fuck's sake, Jacko, that was back in the dark ages. I was barely out of my teens."

"Nothing since then?"

"Royal income tax."

"What?"

"Zero. That's what they pay."

"My, my," said Jacko. He held his glasses towards the light. "Is that how they talk in the entertainment business?"

"A small joke, Jacko, a small joke."

"Like Sainsbury's?"

"That was no joke. That was a cure. That was my little vision on the road to Damascus."

Toaster pushed the ashtray to Jacko's side of the table. Jacko replaced his glasses and picked up the cigar. "Sorry about that." He pushed the handkerchief up his sleeve.

"Three 'ands and an 'andkerchief," said Toaster.

"What?"

"I said I was cured."

"Cured. What happened?"

"You never heard?"

"I heard the odd laugh."

"Oh, it was a great laugh, all right. Twelve hundred quid between three of us."

"It wasn't just the money, though."

"You have heard, then?"

"For God's sake."

"All right, all right, take it easy." Toaster rocked the chair forward onto its two front legs and folded his arms on the table. "There's two of them, the manager and his assistant. The manager's got the briefcase. But not the money. The assistant's got the money. In a carrier bag. Would you believe that? In a carrier bag. A poxy plastic bag advertising margarine or something. And we're too excited –"

Toaster broke off as Goff placed six bottles on the table.

"What price you get?" Goff said to Jacko.

"Five to two. Very nice. It was seven to four at the off. Sit down, Tom. I'm just getting the inside griff on the big supermarket heist."

"Happy days," said Goff, sitting sideways on the chair.

Jacko pointed his cigar at Toaster. "Continue, laddie."

Toaster picked up one of the fresh bottles and filled his glass. "Don't think I'm not onto you bastards."

"Give your tongue some air," said Jacko.

Toaster raised his glass to each of them and drank. "All right, then. Two of them. Manager and assistant. And the assistant's got a plastic carrier bag."

"How many of you?" said Goff.

"There was me and Bandy Richards doing the belabouring and Ray Seddick in the motor. Do you know them?"

Goff shook his head.

"We can't know every clown in town," said Jacko.

"Yeah. Well. They're both inside now," said Toaster. "Which helps keep me smug. Bandy used to suffer from asthma. He sounded like the Flying Scotsman at the best of times. But when he got worked up it was like the Beast from Planet X. He'd keep pulling the mask away to snatch a few heavy lungfuls. Worse than a coal delivery. To top it all, he's getting a bit hysterical on the side. He's whacking the manager and I'm trying to grab the briefcase. But the manager's in a panic and won't let go. Bandy's going uuh, uuh, uuh, and whack, whack, whack. I'm half expecting him to whip out one of those spray jobs and treat himself to a blast of oxygen or whatever it is. I don't know whether to laugh or run. And all the time this assistant's standing there screaming and pushing this carrier bag at me."

"He was offering you the money?"

"Right, right. But I didn't twig. In fact, I turned on the poor bastard and gave him a couple of slaps. I mean, all that hysteria. It's contagious. I could hear him all right. But I wasn't listening. He's shouting, 'Here it is, here's the money, take it, take it,' and I think he's yelling for help. It's not until he sticks his hand in the bag and shoves a handful of readies under my nose that I know what he's on about."

41

"What a farce," said Jacko.

"Hold on, hold on. It gets worse. I finally grab the bag and I'm stuffing the overflow back inside and shouting to Bandy. But he's still whacking away at the manager and the assistant's standing there, his arms wrapped round his head like this, and screaming, 'Stop it, stop it, you've got the money, you've got the money.' And by this time, of course, we've got a bit of an audience as well."

"Applauding, were they?" said Goff.

"Rolling in the gutter. Anyway, I eventually drag Bandy off the manager. And immediately he turns and starts whacking the assistant. Fair play to the man. In the death, though, I get through to him that we've copped the bread. So we both start legging it down to Ray and the motor, about thirty yards away. But just before we get going, the assistant's also on his toes. What a sight it must have been. The manager still lying there, clutching his empty briefcase, and me and Bandy steaming down the road with the assistant a couple of yards in front, looking over his shoulder and putting on a spurt. He thinks we're chasing him, of course. Then just before we reach the motor, Ray leans over and opens the back door. And, would you believe it, the assistant dives into the car."

"Get on," said Jacko.

"Straight. He thinks Seddick's a Samaritan. He's making himself nice and comfy on the back seat, saying 'Thanks, mister, you saved my life' when we pile in on top of him and the motor's away. Well, that must nave been one of the great moments in sport. Ray's up front shouting, 'Who's that cunt? Who's that fucking hitch-hiker?' Bandy's next to me, sounding like he's just about to come. I'm in the middle, pick-axe handle between the knees, money-bag on the lap, with the assistant on the other side looking like a bucket of sick. For all that, I'm nice and cool. I wait until we turn a couple of corners and I say, 'Hold up, Ray,' I say, 'Stop the car.' He says 'What?' So I tell him again. He goes spare. 'This is supposed to be a fucking getaway,' he screams."

"Took umbrage, did he?" said Jacko.

"Umbrage?" said Toaster. "He almost took off through the roof. But he did stop. He probably needed to, all that spit on the windscreen. And I lean over and open the door and say to the assistant, 'You'd better get out.' Poor sod can't believe his luck. 'Sorry,' he keeps saying. 'Awfully sorry.' And finally we're away again. Then Bandy, who by this time's got his breathing back to very heavy, he turns to me and says, 'Who was that?' and I vowed there and then to change my mode of life."

"Mode of life," said Jacko, laughing.

"A very chastening experience," said Goff. He turned to Jacko. "We're leaving after the next race. Going to meet his waiter friend at the Castle. You want to come?"

Jacko looked at his watch. "Aah. Nearly half-past. And I promised to drop some beetroot round to Mary's. The Castle's opposite the sex shop, isn't it?"

"That's right, Jacko," said Toaster. "Only the un-enlightened call it a marriage guidance bureau."

Jacko stubbed his cigar in the ashtray and turned a page of his programme. "What about Dunster's bitch?" he said to Goff.

"What about it?"

"Sammy won't take your bet."

"I'll use cash."

"All right," said Jacko. He stood up and took a roll of money from his pocket. He peeled off five notes and handed them to Goff. "I'll meet you in the pub. If I go straight to Mary's I shouldn't be long behind you."

"Fine," said Goff. He tapped the money against the side of his face and stood up. "I'd better get this down." He jerked his head at Toaster. "Come on, Jesse, watch me make those bookies bleed."

Jacko picked up his programme from the table and turned away. "Within the hour," he said over his shoulder.

"See you later," said Toaster and followed Goff out onto the terracing.

Goff led the way down the aisle to the bookmakers' boards. "You look like a kid at the circus," he said.

"I never liked the circus much," said Toaster. "There was always a funny smell that gave me a headache. The horses bored me and the clowns never made me laugh. But this is something else, Tom. This is real. The very meat of life."

"Mother of God."

"No, I mean it," said Toaster. "A mystical experience. What are you waiting for."

"I'm hoping to get evens. Are you going to have some of this?"

"I've got more respect for money," said Toaster. He tapped his programme. "What about this three dog, Laura's Doom? They're offering thirty-three to one."

Goff moved his mouth to Toaster's ear. "If she was running on her own she'd be third favourite," he whispered.

"She looks good to me."

"I'll give you forty to one."

"I'm tempted."

"No," said Goff. "Save your money. I'll just get this down."

Goff walked into the swarm of gamblers and tic-tac men around the nearest bookmaker and made his wager. He came back to Toaster and kept walking. "Come on, we'll shout her home."

They walked up the terracing to an empty line of seats.

"What price did you get?" said Toaster.

Goff held up his ticket. "Eleven to ten on."

"Which one is it?"

"The two dog."

Down behind the bookmakers the greyhounds were being packed into the boxes.

Goff shook his head. "Did you see those bastards squeeze his balls as he went into the trap?"

"I thought it was a bitch."

"It's those hormone injections, Toaster."

Toaster swung the top half of his body forward and around to look up into Goff's face. "You're tiddly, Goff. How d'you manage that on a few light ales?"

Goff took a flask from his inside pocket and unscrewed the top. "You need a nip of foresight and a dash of enterprise." He topped the flask to his mouth and offered it to Toaster.

The bell rang.

"Is that a warning?" said Toaster. He drank and returned the flask. "Christ, what is it?"

"Moroccan brandy."

Toaster beat his breast with a closed fist.

The traps snapped open and the dogs began the chase. They veered into a bunch at the first bend and the one dog sneaked through on the inside to take a four-length lead.

"Go on the two, go on two, go on two," shouted Toaster.

"She's a little on the deaf side," said Goff. "Give it a touch more lung."

"A touch of Cherry Blossom up the arse more likely," said Toaster.

The one dog held the lead around the final bend and was first past the post with the two dog closing.

Toaster knuckled his eyes. "What colour was that two dog, Tom?"

Goff flicked his ticket away. "It could have been worse."

"How so?"

"I could have been severely embarrassed by Laura's Doom. Come on. Let's get to that pub of yours."

Goff moved into the aisle and down a step. Toaster put a hand on his shoulder. "Now, now, Tom. Laura was fourth. The way you were talking she should just now be coming out of the first bend."

"You're right, Toaster, you're right. It must have been her day."

Goff sat with his back to the tinted windows, watching the pool table.

A redhead, pausing to adjust his glasses after every shot, had sunk five balls in succession. Now he drove the black ball across two cushions and into the middle pocket. His opponent said, "You jammy bastard." The redhead, nicotined fingers chalking the cue, his eyes sliding towards Goff, said, "I had all the luck I needed today when you walked in."

Toaster guided two glasses of whiskey and two pints of Guinness past the pool table and up the steps. He stood holding the glasses in front of Goff, turning his body sideways to allow a packet of crisps to fall to the table from beneath his elbow.

Toaster looked down at the crisps and said, "That's the lunchtime special. Bacon flavoured."

Goff took the two pint mugs from Toaster and set them down. He drank from one and nudged the crisp packet. "I'll leave that there to goad the appetite."

Toaster sat down and placed one of the whiskey glasses in front of Goff. He moved the other pint of Guinness to his own side of the table.

Goff wiped foam from his top lip and waved his glass towards the pool table. "Young Ginger over there can do more with a ball than Mae West."

"Mae who?"

"This place looks ashamed of itself. Last time I was in they had a stage here. And there was a parrot too."

"Captain. Captain John."

"That's right."

"The kids kept feeding him alcohol. Couldn't stop talking, couldn't stay on his perch. He had to go."

Goff stabbed his thumb towards the window. "Did you find out what all the ruckus was about?"

Toaster raised his arm in a Nazi salute. "The fascists. Marching, demonstrating. You know."

"I thought they'd all joined the government."

"Oh, it's bad, Tom. But not bad enough for some."

"And haven't they banned all marches?"

Toaster's face dimpled. "This'll be a spontaneous protest, as they say. Lovely day for a coon hunt, spot of Paki bashing, gob on a kike. And scores of Old Bill to stamp out the retaliation. Do you think Gerry's out there?"

Goff swept his hand through the air. "Never mind Gerry. There'll be more law than order, that's for sure."

"Maybe that's why Jacko's late."

Goff sniffed at his whiskey glass and drank it in one gulp. He poured a half inch of Guinness into the empty glass. "Jacko's always late. He was late for his wedding. You could still smell the puke on his suit. Two months younger than me and he was late for the army. And he missed the sixties altogether. Late in getting away from some tobacco warehouse over Romford way and was allowed eight years to mourn the consequences. And he was late learning to be polite to screws and did every day of it."

"Jeez, I didn't know that. Eight years for a warehouse. Back then?"

"He was late in getting rid of the weight, too."

"Guns? On a warehouse?"

"The security included man-eating Alsatians. Jacko was always fussy about being bitten."

"And he missed the sixties? What a waste."

Goff cupped his hand under his chin and dropped his elbow on the table. "Don't disgust me, Toaster. Eight years inside, that's a waste. But the sixties. What's wrong with you? The sixties. It was all the same old bullshit."

"Come on, Tom, come on. Maybe you were too near to it. Sex, music, hippies, the second Camelot."

"Oh," said Goff, "the second Camelot." He sat erect and drank the Guinness from his whiskey glass. "You mean the Kennedys. Camelot. All right for the knights, maybe, but what about the peasants? That clown Kennedy almost had me killed. And that's the sort of thing I tend to take personally. I remember I changed the kid's prayers. We only had Peter then. He must have been two. After God Bless Mummy and Daddy, I had him say, 'And God bless Nikita Khrushchev, saviour of the world.' It didn't go down well with Marion. She grassed me to Father Doyle who threatened excommunication. He said Tom must be short for tomato seeing I was such a red. A rare wit, he was."

"You'll end up a sour old man, Thomas. Sour and embittered."

Goff smiled and dropped his head. "Ah, maybe you're right, maybe you're right. They say you're getting old when you begin to notice the dog shit in the streets. Though with fifty-four tons of turds a day in London alone, you'd need some pleasant distractions. Myself, I think you're getting old when you go around turning lights out after other people. You doing that yet, Toaster?"

"You mean they don't go off automatically once you leave the room?"

"You'll find out when you're old enough to pay your first bill."

Toaster rapped on the table with his fingers. "There you are, Tom, there you are. You're talking about the sordid green stuff while I'm trying to get a grip on the finer things of life, like brotherly love and cultural freedom. All the things the sixties excelled in."

Goff slid his hands down between his legs, his head near the table. He was looking up and sideways at Toaster, lips parted, his left eye closed. "So, I didn't appreciate the sixties. We're agreed on that. But, tell me this, Toaster, did you ever consider the damage it all caused?"

Toaster laughed. "Go on, go on."

"I was nearly into my twenties when the sixties began.

And I was no late developer. I'd had years of chasing after women. Chasing, mind you. You caught nothing but frustration in those days. It was mooning before and masturbating after."

Toaster raised his hand. "Hold on, hold on. Are you telling me you were a virgin at twenty?"

"I'm telling you nothing of the sort," said Goff. "This is not a personal history. I'm just trying to give you a taste of the times, Toaster. There was a different attitude about. You were coming in your pants if you as much as got your tongue in her mouth." He drank from the Guinness glass and brushed away the foam. "Ah, desperate days indeed. That was nearly all we thought of. A marvellous madness, by God. We had no time for muggings and gang fights and race violence and shoplifting and vandalism. No, no, I'm telling you. There was a bit of it, of course. A bit of everything. But just a bit. Because most of the time we were too busy dreaming and scheming, praying and baying for that elusive cherry. Hold up, now, Toaster. Facts are facts and I was there. As a veteran of the period in question, I'm merely giving you the correct historical perspective."

Toaster laughed, "Jeez, Tom, leave it out."

"As to that, we had very little choice in the matter. But things changed. Oh, how they changed. Women fell from grace in the sixties and they must bear much of the blame for the present sorry state of this once great civilization. They literally fucked our values down the chute."

"So help me, Tom, you'd make a fine preacher."

"Just you look about you, son. It's so bloody easy in this day and age. Almost any young girl'll drop her knickers as long as your teeth aren't green. You've got no worries, no struggle. And all that extra time to make trouble for yourselves and everybody else. If the girls would only keep their jeans zipped up . . . well, you could plot the crime rate by the movement of those zips."

Toaster leaned across the table and tapped Goff on the shoulder. "What are you looking at down there? Keep your eyes on the audience."

Goff raised his head and looked at Toaster. "I was only a couple of years younger than you when they had ration cards. Sweets, bread, meat, clothing, coal. They had ration cards for everything. Except. They had no ration cards for cock, Toaster. And look what a man it made of me."

Goff stood up, looking down at Toaster. He bit his bottom lip. His shoulders quivered. He turned away.

Toaster laughed at the ceiling, striking his fist on the table. "You couldn't keep that old po-face going, could you?"

Goff faced him, smiling. He picked up the Guinness and drained the glass. "Same?"

"Just the stout, Tom. No chaser."

Goff picked up his own whiskey glass and started down the steps. Toaster turned his chair to watch him. Goff paused at the pool table and continued to the bar. He was served at once and carried the three glasses back across the room.

Toaster waited for him to sit down and said, "My God, Tom, you're still very light on your feet. It's years since I saw you and you look as if you haven't had a haircut."

Goff narrowed his eyes and smiled. "You wouldn't be looking for revenge, now, would you, Toaster?"

Toaster threw up both arms. "No, no, straight. You look in really good nick."

"Well, then, if we're exchanging compliments, you've turned into a big strapping lad yourself."

"I've no complaints. But you could still give me three inches and a couple of stone."

Goff dipped his mouth towards the Guinness. "You're on the thin side, right enough. But that's the fashion, is it not? And as for me, lad —" he slapped his rib cage, "well, it's mostly lard."

"There's not enough fat on you to fry an egg. Tell me, Tom, are you still burnishing the Temple of the Lord?"

Goff squeezed his ear lobe and shut his eyes. "My, my, kiddo, you've got one of those memories that terrify your friends. Burnishing, eh? There's them that knocks and them that knows better. As it happens, you've got me in the dock on that one. I've lost my zest of late. Vimmed out, you might say." He pressed his hands into his thighs and crouched forward towards the table. "The last time we met, did we have a drink together?"

"No. It was tea and whist at Aunt Lucy's."

"So. I doubt if you'll catch me doing that again. Nothing against Lucy's tea, you understand. I'm just slipping into bad habits of late. Until a few years ago I had what they call a strong distaste for all forms of alcohol. I'd smoked only one cigarette in my entire life. I used to have a shit every morning at half-past eight and my piss was so pure you could have bottled it and sold it at Lourdes."

"Sacrilege, Thomas. Have you no reverence at all?"

"You'd be better leaving that accent to those misfortunate enough to have no other. Now, where was I?"

"Selling your piss to the pilgrims."

"Just so," said Goff. "Just so." He pulled his chair closer to the table and rested his elbows on top of his thighs. "I could eat anything, any amount, any time. I never gobbed in the gutter like certain parties we won't mention but whose initials are Toaster Kendellan. I never farted either and no one ever had the gall to give me a box of deodorants at Christmas. I had sweet sweat, Toaster, sweet sweat."

"Jesus, Tom, what happened?"

Goff pressed the end of his thumb against the tip of his nose. "It's no great joke, no joke at all. Look at me now. I sometimes need three shits a day. I'm in there so long I'm down to the small ads. And if I try to hurry it up I get spots before my eyes. My piss kills ninety-nine per cent of all household germs and the porcelain is scorched black with the power of it. And that's not all. Along with a weakness for whiskey, I've gone steady on the stout. Which means I fart a lot. I've become a demon at the sly fart, a master of subterfuge, an expert in currents – particularly their response to sudden movement. I know the precise speed, the nice speed, to drift away from the scene of the crime. It takes fine judgement, Toaster, fine judgement."

"Well, it would, it would."

"Indeed. You've got to remove yourself from the ring of suspicion, so to speak, without attracting attention. Or – even more important – without disturbing the delicate balance of natural phenomena controlling the dispersion of lethal gases."

Toaster clapped his hands. "Too much, too much."

Goff looked up at him and shook his head. "Please, now, please."

"You bullshitter, Goff. Too glib, too glib. You're over-rehearsed. You've been practising too much. Without disturbing what?"

Goff said, "Please," and raised his hand. "I was merely saying you shouldn't take it with you when you go."

Toaster, cheeks rosy with drink and laughter, banged his fist on the table. "You've worn out the mirror, Tom, worn out the mirror."

Goff took two mouthfuls of Guinness and spoke to the glass. "Well now, I won't deny that this farting business has been monopolizing my waking thoughts just lately. I'm getting a new insight into corruption." He shook his head at the glass and switched his eyes to Toaster. "First the gut, then the nose. And finally, God help us, the brain itself. The bastards grow on you, Toaster. They slake a secret longing, something primeval. It's a lonely field of research, mind. It's not something you can share. But the rewards, Toaster, the rewards. I lie in bed of a morning and savour the night's work. A gentle waft of the sheets and it comes slithering out of the bed like a suppressed sin. Dirty but delicious. It's addictive. I've become a fart junkie."

"Masterful, Thomas, masterful. You're talking to a convert," said Toaster. He held up his glass. "And you couldn't get better raw material."

"A terrible price, though," said Goff. "I can feel the body disintegrating, week by week."

"Ah, bad, bad booze."

"It's the rope that breaks your neck but the crime that gets you hung," said Goff.

"What?"

"The booze is just the means, Toaster. I'm the victim of tragic circumstances. A fallen paragon. You asked about the temple because you see it crumbling into ruin. But it would be as good as ever, glowing with vigour, if it hadn't been for this terrible catastrophe that overwhelmed the world, that set —"

"You mean the Second World War?"

Goff shifted his body from side to side and tapped his index finger against his chin. "Well, now, if you're going to be facetious, Toaster."

Toaster cut his hand through the air. "My apologies, Tom. A poor jest. The stout's out. Tear ahead, there's a good man."

Goff lounged forward again, elbows on thighs. "Pay close attention then because my suspicions are aroused. Mark this. There's only one way to burnish the temple. One way." He sat upright and struck his index finger against the edge of the table to emphasize the words. "First. Class. Maintenance. Constant. Regular. Servicing. And you know what that means, Toaster, d'you know?"

"I don't, Tom."

"It means exercising. Exercising. Not your thirty press-ups every morning, knees-bend-touch-the-toes crap. None of your bathroom bicycles and rowing machines. You've got to get out there and stretch the legs. You've got to run, you've got to blow, you've got to be out there in the park. Just you, God, and maybe the milkman. Before the birds and the frost are up. Before the dogs have shattered the grass with mines. Not bad, that. Before the sun in winter. There's nothing like it, Toaster. It's like rape of the morning, kicking that dew out of bed. I loved it. I did it for years. Rain, snow, fog, mist or sunshine – spring was always in the air."

"Very nicely put, Tom."

Goff blew air through his fluted bottom lip. "If your mouth ran on petrol, there'd be no oil glut."

"Even better, Tom. Tart."

"Do you want me to start sulking, Toaster?"

"What? And never learn about this terrible catastrophe? Please."

"Just so, then. Back to the dance among the daffodils. The truth of the matter is, Toaster, the truth is I never realized how good I had it. Took it all for granted like a sound belch." He moved closer to the table and dropped his voice. "And then one day I was not alone. There ahead of me, taking my dew, so to speak, were two other runners. Athletes, I thought. Until I got close up. Legs on them, Toaster, legs on them like a mended vase. You could take a canoe down their varicose veins. By the end of the week, it wasn't two, it was a dozen. And by the end of the month, it was metropuke. That park was like the Piccadilly overspill. You know what it was? You know what it was? Some cranky Yank was urging the world to take up jogging. Joggers. Jesus, Mary and Joseph, Toaster, you couldn't invent a more disgusting sight. Thousands upon thousands of them. All ages, all sexes, cripples and half-wits, coughing and wheezing, spitting and gasping, going pale and purple, running rainbows they were, throwing thrombos all round me."

"Running rainbows," said Toaster, slapping the table.

"It's God's truth," said Goff. "Obscene is what it was. A fashion parade. Tracksuits and headbands and cut-away silk shorts and running shoes with little emblems."

"And stopwatches, Tom. Don't forget the watches."

"Yes, watches, too. You're right. And the ugliness. Blotchy skin and running noses, drooling mouths, big steaming thighs juggling seven layers of fat. Now I've got a strong stomach, Toaster – at least, I did then – and I could live with that. The eyes winced a bit, no doubt, but I could stay alive. No, what killed me was their conceit. Where they panted, I purred. And they couldn't tell the difference. No respect. No respect at all. I hesitate to tell you this, Toaster, but they thought I was one of themselves. They had the gall to talk to me as if we all belonged to some elite little club, as if I read their smart Sunday newspapers and could be taken in by the latest fad. Jesus, they probably thought I was trendy."

"The sauce, Tom. The bloody sauce. You soon sorted out that line of chat, I trust?"

"It wasn't a line, it was a wave, a typhoon. They destroyed me, Toaster. They destroyed me with intimacy. Little waves, knowing smirks, smug good-mornings. And they had a cat's-piss way of talking, 'burning the blubber' and 'breaking through the barrier', that took the enamel off my teeth. I tried everything. Other parks, other schedules. To no avail. The world was awash with joggers. I was routed, Toaster, driven gibbering from the field, my temple doomed to inevitable decay."

"A catastrophe indeed, Tom. A lesson to us all. But the man's dead now. The cranky Yank. Plucked away in mid-stride, pounding his way around the clouds. The parks are yours again. Return and rebuild the old glory."

Goff took four long swallows from his Guinness glass. "No, no, the rhythm's broken. And besides, there's been some compensation. I've developed an awful case of ESP since I stopped the running, Toaster."

"You have? How d'you mean?"

"I'll show you if I can. This mate of yours, the waiter. Fix him in your mind."

"Graham?"

"Yes, imagine him sitting here."

"All right."

Goff closed his eyes and pressed both hands to his temples. "He's about five-nine, slim, black hair, oily black hair. And very pale-skinned. I see him wearing one of those blue canvas jackets and jeans. He's the nervous type, restless."

Toaster looked over his shoulder. Beasley was sitting alone at the table adjacent to the main doors. He raised his left hand to Toaster.

"You clever bastard," Toaster laughed, sweeping Goff's hands away from his face. "How did you know it was him?"

"Who?"

"You might be able to sell the Virgin Mary a packet of three but you can't fool me, Goff."

"That's not good talk, Toaster."

"You're not getting religious on me, are you?"

"You don't have to be religious to know that's not good talk."

"All right, I'm sorry, Tom. But how did you know?"

"What's his name again?"

"Graham Beasley."

"He's been sitting there a few minutes, looking over this way. I figured he was just too shy to burst in on us."

"Right. Will I bring him over or do you want to wait for Jacko?"

"Jacko might be tomorrow. I'll give Mary a ring, find out what's happened to him." Goff stood up and held out a note towards Toaster. "Fetch the lad over and fetch a fresh round of drinks while you're down that way."

"It's my shout," said Toaster.

"Take the money, man. You don't earn grace from that sort of suffering."

"I'm not counting the rounds, Tom."

Goff laughed. "We all know that, Toaster."

"And what does that mean?"

Goff spread his hands. "Come on now, Toaster. You'll say worse to me today and I won't give you a look as hard as that one."

Toaster smiled and took the money. "I will too, you bastard. I'll work on it."

Goff replaced the telephone receiver and ducked his head to look through the square of glass in the door of the booth. Toaster, talking and twirling his right hand, was sitting at the table with Beasley.

Goff took out his handkerchief, covered his little finger and probed his ear. He examined the handkerchief, switched hands and probed the other ear. He put the handkerchief away and stepped out of the booth.

Toaster stopped talking and pushed his chair back as Goff approached the table. "Graham," he said, "This is my Uncle Tom. Tom, Graham Beasley."

Goff shook hands. "Hello, Graham."

"Pleased to meet you, Mr Goff."

"Tom's better."

"D'you get him?" said Toaster.

"Engaged," said Goff. He sat down. "We'll give it a few minutes."

"We were just talking about queues," said Toaster.

"Buses or billiard balls?"

"Hee, hee, hee. Lines of people, Thomas."

"If you're in a queue, you're in the wrong place," said Goff.

"Yes, that's good. But what if there's nothing else but queues?" said Beasley.

"Like where?"

"Like the social security offices. I was there this morning with my sister. You get a ticket when you go in and wait till your number flashes up over one of the booths. Her number was 243. They were on 81 when we sat down."

"But what a floor show," said Toaster, pushing Goff's change across the table. "He was just telling me."

"Cemeteries," said Goff. "That's where you go to bury your dignity."

"Don't tell me you've ever been to the dole office, Tom," said Toaster.

"We've all got sisters."

Beasley settled his elbows on the armrests and intertwined his fingers across his stomach. "I know I was laughing about it, Toaster, the shouting and screaming, the wingeing kids, the bullshit, the madness. But it's pretty fucking depressing. Damp pushchairs."

"Yes," said Goff. "Damp pushchairs. And carrycots. Piss-stained carrycots."

"And despair leaking out of people as they come apart before your eyes," said Beasley.

"He's a poet, this man," Goff said to Toaster.

"A romantic," said Toaster. "I used to be a romantic till I fell in love."

"Half an hour down the SS and you'd be a communist," said Beasley.

Goff picked up his whiskey glass and held it to the light. "What sort of drink is this, Toaster?"

"It's a triple, Tom. The least I could get you."

Goff sipped his drink. "Every hour or so, there's a great lesson to be learnt from life," he said to Beasley. "And it's usually: it's later than you think."

"What does that mean?" said Toaster.

"Enjoy yourself. It's an old song."

"What you say is true. But it's too hard," said Beasley. "There's lots of things to know. Big things like you're going to die, like you really know nothing. But you can't live like that. With those things in mind all the time, I mean. It's too hard."

"A philosopher, too," said Goff.

"There's greater reason than reason," said Toaster.

"The drink makes your dimples dance, Toaster," said Goff. He smiled at Beasley. "Just a foxtrot at the moment. When it becomes a cha-cha-cha we start to worry."

58

Beasley stretched forward to pick up his half-pint glass. "You're blanking me, aren't you?" he said to Goff.

"What?"

"You're blanking me."

Goff looked at Toaster.

Toaster shook his head. "I haven't said a word."

"That's right, he hasn't," said Beasley. He raised his glass to Goff. "Thanks for the drink."

Goff nodded his head. "You don't waste much time on small talk, do you?"

Beasley emptied his glass, placed it back on the table and hunched his shoulders. "That's a line of small talk, wouldn't you say?"

"Christ."

Toaster touched Beasley's arm with his elbow. "Hey, take it easy, Graham."

"Don't worry, I'm easy. I'm a pessimist. It lessens the pain."

"You sound a mite bitter to me," said Toaster.

Beasley folded his arms. "Well, you can prepare yourself for a blank. It's the soft-soap that sticks in the craw."

"You are a friend of Toaster's?" said Goff.

"So what?"

"I wouldn't soft-soap a friend of Toaster's no matter what sort of snotty attitude he brought to my table."

Beasley looked at Goff and his eyes began to blink. He looked at Toaster and back to Goff. "Look, if I'm out of order, I'm sorry. I didn't mean it to sound bad. This is important to me, that's all. And you are saying no, aren't you?"

"He is a friend of yours, isn't he, Toaster?"

Toaster put his hand on Beasley's shoulder. "We scrumped apples together."

Beasley moved forward in his chair towards Goff. "Look –" he began.

Goff stopped him with a sweep of his left hand, the open palm close to Beasley's face. He held his left hand there and drank whiskey with his right. "Tell me if I'm wrong," he said. He took another drink of whiskey, emptying the glass, and dropped both hands beneath the table onto his thighs. "You've got a bent friend in the CID, that right? This jack drops the word that fourteen kilos of cocaine will be coming into London Airport, that's Heathrow, on the twenty-ninth. Some time between nine and ten o'clock at night. Yes? The customs know it's coming so they're going to grab it. And they've decided – because it's so valuable and because so much has been disappearing from their own store – they've decided to stash it overnight at the Uxbridge nick. All right so far?"

Beasley nodded. "That's about it."

"Good," said Goff. "And the customs don't trust the law, either, never mind their own people. So they'll only leave it in the nick that one night. Next day it'll be carted off to the Tower of London or whatever. Yes?"

"As far as I know."

"Okay. So you think, I'll have some of this, and get in touch with Toaster. Because Toaster knows us. But you don't know us, Graham. And it shows."

"How do you mean."

Goff sat up in his chair and rubbed both hands across his face. "What plane is this stuff coming in on?"

"I don't know."

"No. You don't know. You didn't even bother to check the flights before spewing off with this cocaine shit. There's a very limited number of flights into Heathrow at night, Graham. The local residents have seen to that. There's none from South America and none from North America after ten past eight on the twenty-ninth. Now where else would that amount of cocaine be coming from?"

"I don't know."

"Well, now, did you know this? There's a flight from Pakistan scheduled to arrive at nine-fifteen that night?"

"No, I didn't."

"But it doesn't surprise you, does it, Graham? Because if anything is coming in that night, it's heroin, not cocaine."

Beasley smiled and allowed his body to sag back into his chair. He opened his hands to Toaster. "Hey, come on. Is that the big complaint? He said 'gear' or 'powder'. Maybe I jumped to conclusions when I said cocaine. But what difference does it make? It's more or less the same price. And it's bound to be top quality."

Goff turned away from the table, shaking his head. "Can the bullshit."

"What bullshit?"

"The what-difference-does-it-make bullshit. If there's no difference, why did you say cocaine?"

"I told you. I just assumed it was. Anyway, Toaster takes the odd line and I knew he'd realize its value."

Goff turned to Toaster. "Is that right?"

"What?"

"You take that crap?"

"Only when it's free, Thomas."

Goff drank from his Guinness glass. "All right, Graham, I'll tell you what difference it makes and then you can go home and tell your mother how to change a nappy. The difference, Graham, is public opinion. Heroin's got a dirty reputation. It frightens people. It even frightens drug-takers. And I know it frightens judges just by reading the papers and the sentences they hand out."

"It frightens you, too, does it?"

"You're not really listening, are you, Graham?"

"If I thought we were going to get caught, I wouldn't be sitting here."

Goff looked at Toaster and pressed the tip of his nose with his thumb. He picked up the pint of Guinness and drained it. He tapped the empty glass on the table. "Toaster, any chance of another growl?"

"Sure, Tom," said Toaster, standing up. "I was waiting for a chance. Same again?"

"Just a small whiskey this time."

"And what about you, big mouth?" Toaster said to Beasley.

"Just a half, please."

Goff waited until Toaster had descended into the well

of the bar. He rested his elbows on the table and pointed the index finger of his right hand at Beasley. "You listen to me, Mr Beasley. This job's a no-no. You understand that? It's got more holes than a golf course. That means we're not interested. That means Toaster's not interested. If I hear anything different, I'll come looking for you."

Beasley held both hands, palms open, at his shoulders. "Just a minute. Now just a minute, Mr Goff. Let's get this right. Toaster was never in the frame on this one. That was decided from the start. And there's no need for threats. If you say no, that's it. That's it. Honestly, you've got it wrong. And I wasn't really trying to con you. I had no idea you were so pissed off at heroin."

Goff arced his thumb upwards until his pointing finger became a gun. He retracted his finger and closed his fist. "That's good." He shifted his body away from the table and dropped his elbows back onto his thighs. He hung his head and tapped his feet. He looked up at Beasley. "Maybe I'm being a bit hard on you, Graham. You've no idea how bad this sounds to me. And I'm not pissed off at heroin. Personally, I don't give a shit. If people want to take this drug that's up to them. It would be all right with me if it was given away with washing powder. But that's just me. You've got to understand that, about public opinion. Most people have got a big emotional thing about heroin. It gets a lot of bad publicity and they get all excited. They think it kills, turns kids into monsters. They think it's depraved, Graham. Depraved. Now, I can see you're ready to tell me it's the public who are turned into monsters and maybe you're right."

"It's not that exactly but if you'll just listen for –"

Goff held up his hand. "No. You listen. I don't want you to tell me what I already know. And I don't want you repeating back to me what I'm telling you either. So listen, all right?"

"I'm listening. I'm listening."

"What we've got here is an emotional problem. You're right when you say the street price per gramme is more or less the same as coke. But we're talking about wholesale so I went to see a certain party and asked what sort of price we might get for fourteen kilos of good cocaine. He mentioned a very handsome sum indeed. I'm very interested. I make further inquiries. I check the flights and it's obvious that it's got to be heroin. So, I go back to this certain party and I say sorry, it's heroin, not cocaine. And you know what he told me, Graham? He told me to get the fuck out of his office. 'Heroin,' he said, 'is just a headache.' He advised me to leave it to the foreigners. The Chinks, the Iranians, the Pakis. If I liked, he'd put me in touch with someone who'd take it off my hands. But at a much lower price. About a quarter of what you'd get for the coke. From people who'd steal the eye out of a storm so I'd have to spend more time and money protecting myself. And then he gave me a big lecture about the business –"

"Who'd dare to lecture you, Tom?" said Toaster, standing over the table with the drinks.

Goff took a whiskey and a pint of Guinness from Toaster. "Nobody you know."

Toaster gave Beasley his half pint of bitter and sat down. "Lecturing you about dope, was he?"

"About heroin," said Goff. "About what a messy business it was. About public emotions. About stiff sentences."

"What about the Bolivian nose-bleed?" said Toaster.

"He said cocaine was easy. A smart people's drug, non-addictive. He said the middle classes lap it up, buy it in large quantities. Cocaine, he said, you can sell by the ounce. It's the people with money who indulge. They can take cocaine and go on working. They can take cocaine and not feel guilty. They can take cocaine and boast about it. People who take heroin don't have a lot of money. Apparently, if you take heroin you can't work. Or you don't want to work. So nobody buys an ounce. They can't afford an ounce. They buy a gramme or even a bag so it's harder to unload. He also said people who take heroin don't boast about it. They become ashamed of themselves. Is that right, Graham?"

"Hey," said Beasley. He rolled back his sleeve to expose his left arm. "Look at that. Clean as a whistle."

"You never tried it, Gray?" said Toaster.

"I've snorted it once or twice. It just made me sick."

"Anyway, Graham," said Goff. "You understand what I'm saying? Why we can't do business?"

"You've been very straight," said Beasley. "I appreciate that."

"No hard feelings, then?" said Goff, holding his hand across the table.

Beasley shook hands. "Of course not. I'm just sorry it didn't work out. Just one thing, though. I hope you don't think I was trying a con. Not with Toaster involved, I mean."

"Leave it out, Beasley," said Toaster.

"Look, Graham," said Goff. "Even if I was sure it was cocaine, I'd leave it alone. The whole thing reeks to me. But if you're determined to push ahead there are people who might be interested."

"You mean south of the river?"

"It's a possibility."

Beasley shook his head. "Thanks anyway. The only thing I'd take over there is a hungry horse."

"That's true," said Goff. "Good grazing. You'd be well advised to take a close look at that jack, too. They can be devious bastards."

"Oh, I know that, I know that," said Beasley. "But this is kosher. In the first place I know the bloke quite well. If he nicks anybody with dope, smoke, you know, he sells me what the analyst don't get. Which is most of it. And, in the second place –" Beasley turned to Toaster. "Have you told him about the ear?"

"Jesus, no," said Toaster. He smiled at Goff. "You've got to see this, Tom. It's unbelievable. Come on, Graham, give us a demo."

"Take it easy, Toaster," said Beasley. He spoke to Goff. "You know I'm a waiter? At Carson's?"

"I've heard," said Goff. "Fancy joint. Swallow anything but the prices."

"Credit-card cuisine," said Toaster. "If you pay with money, you're dirt. The type that blows his nose in the napkin."

"Keep it down, Toaster," said Goff.

"Let's play whispers," said Toaster, his voice hushed.

"What's this ear?" Goff said to Beasley.

Beasley turned his head into profile and squeezed and wriggled the lobe of his left ear. "It's the waiter's secret weapon. If you're good you can pick up a conversation across seven or eight tables, working tables that is, with twenty or thirty people clashing away in top gear. It's just a knack you get for filtering out all the other noises. And I'm the Jodrell Bank of the profession. I tell you, Mr Goff, if you eat at my place just remember a whisper is an indiscretion."

"My, my," said Goff.

"That's not bullshit," said Beasley.

"I tell you, Tom, he's unbelievable."

"Aren't we all?" Goff said to Toaster. "Does that make me deaf?" He crouched in towards Beasley. "And that's how you heard of the shipment, is it?"

"Right," said Beasley. "This detective, Hicks his name is, he eats at our place. He pays, too. I just bung him some blank bills for his expenses."

"Everyone's at it," said Toaster.

"Please, Toaster," said Beasley. "This Hicks. About a month ago he has lunch with this big-noise from the customs. An inspector. Inspector Nelson. What a slur on the glory of old England. Anyway, Nelson tells Hicks about the bust they're going to have. He wants to know what sort of reward he can expect for syphoning off a few ounces. They're talking hush-hush but I've got the old ear working. Not that I need to actually. Because afterwards Hicks hangs around to have a word with me. Would I be interested in five ounces of good gear? That's when I got the brilliant idea of grabbing the lot before any of the Bill start copping their share."

"This Nelson," said Toaster. "Was he chancing his arm or just turning a blind eye?"

"Oh, my God," said Beasley.

"Dry, Toaster, dry but melting," said Goff.

"Remember my condition, Thomas. Not bad under the circumstances."

"You're going to need grub or you'll be laming us," said Goff. He pushed the packet of crisps towards Toaster. "Start on these. I'll give Jacko another bell and then we'll go and eat. What about you, Graham? Do you fancy –" Goff broke off, looking beyond Beasley to the main doors. "Looks like some of the marchers have decided on a detour."

Toaster and Beasley turned their heads. Five young men with close-cropped hair were clustered in the well of the bar. Three wore chain-worked leather jackets. The other two had anoraks decorated with Union Jacks. One spoke to the barman and they all left through the side door leading to the toilets and the public bar.

"Not selling the *War Cry*," said Toaster.

"Did you see that swastika tattooed on his head?" said Beasley.

"Hello, hello, hello," said Goff. "Here comes the cavalry."

A policeman had entered the bar. He looked around and approached the barman.

"Fucking hell," said Beasley. "It's one of the Oafs."

"What happened to pigs?" said Goff.

Beasley shook Toaster's forearm. "That's Kilbride. You've heard of the Oafs?"

Toaster pulled his arm free. "Take it easy, Graham. No, I haven't. What's wrong with you? He's leaving anyway."

The policeman had moved away from the barman, walking back to the main doors. He pushed the door ajar with his foot, holding it there, adjusting his tie. He turned and touched his helmet to the barman and walked into the street.

"We ought to get out of here," said Beasley.

"Sit tight," said Goff. "He's likely a ferret flushing rabbits. Maybe those kids."

Toaster laughed and squeezed Beasley's shoulder. "Badgers don't bolt. What are you getting excited about, Gray?"

"You just don't know, do you?" said Beasley. "He's one of the Oafs. They're the cunts who dropped that black kid onto the railings a couple of weeks ago. You didn't hear about that?"

"Left-wing propaganda," said Toaster. "The bleeding hearts' bible. Our boys in blue are wonderful, Graham. Ask anyone."

"Who are they?" said Goff.

Beasley hunched into the table, wrapping both hands around his drink. "You know those mobile patrol units? They're one of them. Most of those units, ten men in a van cruising around looking for trouble, most of them have got a sergeant in charge. This one's got Inspector William George Grace. W. G. Grace. Got it?"

Goff looked at Toaster. Toaster pulled his mouth askew and shrugged.

"I'm sorry, Graham," said Goff.

"W. G. Grace. He was a famous cricketer. This W. G. Grace, this Inspector, he's a famous fuck-up. He can't wipe his arse without a mirror. They call him W. G. Oaf at the nick. That's what his own people call him. His own people. Christ. Haven't you two ever heard of W. G. Grace?"

"Kept a straight bat, did he?" said Toaster.

"The man's a bloody legend."

"Couldn't walk, though, could he?" said Toaster. "I think I read somewhere that he couldn't walk."

"What?"

"Relax, Graham," said Toaster. "We're only teasing. I always felt there was something slightly anti-social about cricket. You were never any good, Beasley. You used to duck out of the way in the slips."

"I like to watch, though."

"Do you remember batting?" said Toaster. "And your partner at the other end was out? Even if you liked the bloke, do you remember secretly feeling a bit pleased?

Especially if he got a duck. That way it wouldn't be so bad for you if –"

"I knew it," interrupted Beasley, looking over his shoulder. "I knew it. We should have scarpered."

The policeman, Kilbride, had re-entered the bar. Close behind him came two more policemen, both without helmets. They stood together, just inside the open door, looking back into the street.

"There's no Inspector there," said Goff.

"No, he ain't there," said Beasley. "He probably got lost on the way in. Still trying to slide open the swing doors."

Toaster laughed. "That's oafully funny, Graham."

Beasley covered his bottom lip with his teeth and moved his chair sideways. "These dickheads are no joke, Toaster. Keep it down."

"Now come on, Graham."

"I'm telling you. The one with the spiky hair and the sergeant's stripes. That's Swakely. He's the brains of the outfit. And they all think intelligence is a criminal offence. Watch Kilbride, too. He's as thick as fourteen lavatory seats and just as awkward. If he tried to pick his nose he'd miss his face."

"What about the other one?" said Goff.

Beasley shook his head. "I don't know them all. They change them around. Swakely and Kilbride are well known. They've even had their pictures in the local paper." He stiffened and clutched at Goff's upper arm. "There he is now. That's him."

The door leading to the toilets and the public bar swung open and four more policemen, led by an officer with a peaked cap, came into the saloon. The officer carried a wooden baton. He tapped it against his neck as he crossed the room to speak to Sergeant Swakely.

"That's the prick," said Beasley. "The cunt with the stick."

All the customers in the lounge, including the pool players, turned to look at the group of seven policemen. In the silence, Sergeant Swakely's voice carried across the room. "He says nobody."

68

Grace scanned the tables, tapping his foot against the floor and the stick against his neck. "Check them anyway," he said, his voice loud, his baton stick sweeping around the room.

"All right," said Swakely to the other policemen. "Get them all down here."

Swakely himself moved to the pool table. He snatched the cue from one of the players and threw it on the table. "Get down there," he said, gesturing towards the toilets.

Grace stood watching near the door as the policemen herded the customers away from the tables.

Kilbride had moved past the pool table and up the steps towards Goff, Toaster and Beasley.

"Sharpish," Swakely called up to him.

Kilbride put his hand behind Beasley's neck and squeezed. "What sergeant says, sergeant means," he said. He was smiling at Goff and Toaster over Beasley's head.

Goff stood up, rocking his chair. Kilbride released Beasley and stepped back. He was still smiling. He raised an index finger and tapped his nose at Goff.

Toaster stood and touched Goff on the shoulder. "Easy, Tom."

"That's right, Tom. You take it easy," said Kilbride. He looked behind him, feeling for the top step with the heels of his boot. He clapped his hands and rubbed them together. "All right, comrades, let's move it, shall we?"

Beasley made a popping noise with his mouth and levered himself up from his chair, his hands flat on the table. He walked down the steps and past the pool table. Sergeant Swakely, his buttocks hitched over the corner pocket, pushed him in the back as he passed. "Come on, come on."

Goff kissed his teeth and picked up his whiskey glass. "A bunch of actors," he said to Toaster.

"What's that, dad? What did you say?" said Kilbride.

Goff made a sudden movement with his right hand. Kilbride swayed backwards. Goff continued the movement, bringing the glass to his lips and emptying it. He snapped it back on the table, upside down. "Dregs," he said. "Just the dregs."

Toaster smiled. "After you, Thomas," he said, flourishing his right arm towards the steps.

Goff looked at Kilbride and ran his tongue around his lips. He stepped past Toaster and descended the steps, forcing Kilbride to move aside.

Toaster picked up the packet of crisps from the table and followed him.

Sergeant Swakely had stayed by the pool table, rolling a cue backwards and forwards across the cloth with his left hand. As Goff drew abreast of him, he picked up the cue and struck Goff across the back of the head.

"Tom," shouted Toaster, lunging forward. He was tripped by Kilbride.

Goff staggered under the blow and tried to turn. The sergeant moved after him and struck again with the thick, heavy end of the cue. Goff grunted and stumbled into the bar, collapsing on his hands and knees, rolling his head. Swakely stood over him and hit him a third time between the neck and shoulders. Goff's right arm lost its tension and his body slid sideways into the foot-rest.

Toaster, struggling to rise, was repeatedly kicked by Kilbride in the groin and stomach. The crisp packet burst apart with a wheezing pop and the crisps flaked across Toaster's chest. He rolled beneath the pool table, clutching his stomach.

"Nice one, sarge," Kilbride said to Swakely. He bent to stretch his hand beneath the pool table, took a grip on the collar of Toaster's coat and dragged him into the middle of the bar.

Inspector Grace left the customers lined up against the far wall and walked across to Toaster. His eyes lingered on Goff and switched to the sergeant. "What's going on?"

The sergeant tapped the cue on the floor and nodded his head towards Goff. "I gave the big fella a taste of this."

"What happened?" said Grace.

The sergeant moved the ball of his thumb across the tip of the cue. "I didn't like the way he looked at Will."

"I didn't like it much either," said Kilbride. He stepped towards Goff and looked down into his face. "No, I didn't." He jabbed the heel of his boot into Goff's cheekbone. Goff's head rebounded from the foot-rest.

"Why didn't you use your truncheon?" Grace said to the sergeant.

Swakely sighed. "Lost it, ain't I?"

"Have you reported it?"

"Yes, I have. And two pairs of cuffs. And a box of cigars. And a new squash racket. There's been more pricks in my locker than Fanny Hill."

Grace jiggled the baton against his neck. "Well, get it replaced. You can't expect a snooker cue to be handy every time you have to hit somebody."

Toaster rolled onto his back, his mouth open, dragging at air, his eyes nearly closed. "No reason. Cowardly shitheads."

Kilbride grinned down at him. "Lively bugger, this one." He bent his knees and spread his left hand on Toaster's chest. "Lively little darling, ain't you, dearie?" He drove his right fist into Toaster's solar plexus.

Toaster's head jerked forward and he tried to turn his body. A cone of vomit spurted from his mouth and splattered across the boots and trousers of both Kilbride and Grace.

"Bastard," screamed Kilbride, leaping backwards. He stepped back towards Toaster and swung his right boot.

Grace pushed Kilbride aside, swinging him back into the pool table.

"You disgusting sod," Grace shouted at Toaster. He wiped the cap of his left boot on Toaster's coat. "Clean it up, you scumbag. Clean it up."

Toaster opened his eyes, coughed, sucked in air and tried to spit at Grace. The brown spittle dribbled down his chin.

Kilbride kicked him in the groin. Toaster gargled. Vomit ran from his nose. His body arced and his head snapped back against the floor.

Grace stabbed his baton into Kilbride's shoulder. "I

said leave him to me. Don't you understand that? Leave him to me." Loose crisps crunched beneath his feet.

"All right, all right," said Kilbride. "I just thought –"

"Shut up, Will," said Swakely.

Grace took hold of Toaster's hair with his left hand and dragged him clear of the vomit. He shook Toaster's head backwards and forwards by the hair. "Can you hear me, fartface? I'll teach you something. I'll teach you some respect."

Grace placed his left boot on the side of Toaster's neck and threaded the baton through the loop of the gold ring on Toaster's right ear. He removed his foot, released Toaster's hair and jerked at the baton. "Up, up, up."

Toaster's right hand fumbled at the baton. Grace jerked and pulled, dragging Toaster towards the bar.

The ring came away from the ear in a blur of blood and flesh.

Grace, unbalanced, fell against the bar, the baton held high. The ear-ring tingled down the stick to leave a purple smear on his gloved thumb.

Blood poured from Toaster's ear, down the side of his neck and beneath the collar of his shirt.

Grace twirled the ring up and down the baton and turned to face the bar. "Give me a clean glass," he said to the barman. He looked around at Sergeant Swakely and raised the baton. "Self-mutilation, and we'll keep the evidence."

Swakely smiled and rubbed his chin. "You tried to stop him, guv, but it was all over in a flash."

Kilbride laughed.

Grace turned back to the bar and extended his left hand to the barman. "Where's that glass?"

"What sort do you want?"

"A small one. Any sort, for crying out loud."

Grace looked down at Goff who had pushed himself away from the foot-rest. He was on his hands and knees, grunting with each breath.

"Shut your noise," Grace said to him.

Goff shook his head and looked sideways at Toaster,

face white, smeared with blood and vomit, eyes closed, lying on the floor. Goff leaned his body to the right, balanced himself on his right hand and swung his left, fingers stiff and squared away, an upward jab, into Grace's kidneys.

Grace sagged and paled. His eyes protruded. He dropped the baton and the ring onto the top of the bar.

Goff swung again at the same spot. As he struck, he grunted and slipped, catching Grace's trousers at shin height to retain his balance.

Grace's knees bent and he swayed into the bar. His head dropped forward and his hat fell off. His hands scrabbled for support and swept the baton off the bar. It fell to the floor and bounced from the foot-rest.

The ring rolled free.

One of the policemen stepped past Grace and brought his truncheon down across the back of Goff's neck. He pitched forward, his left arm twisting behind him. The policeman hit him a second blow and raised his arm for a third.

He was impeded by Grace buckling sideways, his chin clipping the edge of the bar, his legs collapsing, kneeling on the foot-rest until the whole body toppled and slumped. He lay face up on the floor, his face grey against a balloon of blood from a bitten lip, his head touching the back of Goff's right knee.

"Blimey," said Swakely. He bent and eased his hands under Grace's armpits. "Give us a hand."

The policeman who had hit Goff dropped his truncheon and straightened Grace's legs.

"Gently," said the sergeant, lifting Grace into a sitting position.

Grace's closed eyes were wet. Bubbles of sweat blistered on his forehead.

Kilbride sniggered and the sergeant looked at him. Kilbride shrugged and said, "He'll piss blood for a week."

"He looks ready to cash in," said the policeman at his feet.

"Don't talk stupid," said Swakely. "You were a bit slow there, weren't you?"

"He took me by surprise. Anyway, Will was nearer."

"Bollocks," said Kilbride. "I was watching the honker."

"Cut it out," said Swakely. He looked up at the other officers. "What the fuck are you all staring at? Swan, give Evans a hand. Here, take this end. Get him into the public bar on that long seat. And be careful."

The two policemen carried Grace through the toilet door. The sergeant tapped Kilbride on the arm and gestured at the customers huddled against the wall. "Get those clowns out of here. Is the public cleared?"

"Yes, sergeant," said one of the policemen.

"Shall I call a doctor?" said Kilbride.

"Let's see what a brandy does for him first."

"This one needs a doctor more," said the policeman standing over Toaster. "He's lost a lot of blood."

The sergeant crossed to Toaster and looked down at him. "Florence fucking Nightingale," he said to the policeman. "Nobody's touching either of these jokers until W.G.'s had a chance to thank them personally."

"He was with them," said Kilbride, pointing at Beasley.

"Yeah? Keep him too, then. Get the others out and the doors locked. And no more fuck-ups, please," said Swakely, pushing through the toilet door.

Kilbride walked to the wall and took Beasley by the shoulder. "Over there, sunshine. With your mates. The rest of you can take off."

One of the other officers held the main doors open for the customers to file out. He locked it behind them.

Beasley had not moved. Kilbride took his shoulder again and escorted him towards Goff and Toaster. "Hey, Sully," he called to the policeman at the door. "Maybe you'd better get some cuffs on King Kong here. Before he wakes up and bites your head off."

"What about the other one?"

Kilbride bent over to examine Toaster and prodded

74

him with his boot. "You awake, Van Gogh? No, I wouldn't bother. He looks bad enough to me. You there. What's your name?"

"Beasley."

"Beasley what?"

"Graham Beasley."

"All right, Graham, get some water from behind the bar and clean your mate up. Try and stop that bleeding. You his boyfriend, are you?"

"What's that supposed to mean?"

"Ah, well, I don't blame you. If he drips away like this for another ten minutes even Dracula won't fancy him."

"He needs a doctor," said Beasley. "You should call an ambulance. They both need medical treatment."

Kilbride walked up to Beasley until they were almost touching. "But you don't, do you? And, if I was you, I'd remember why."

Beasley, slouched into the dashboard, face cupped in the heels of his hands, hissed through his teeth.

Toaster sat up and leaned over the steering wheel. "What is it?"

"He's coming back."

"Where? I can't see anything."

"I've lost him again. He was looking at their car. He's sweet on his feet."

"Sweet sweat," said Toaster. He moved across to the middle of the seat and lowered the radio.

"Come again," said Beasley.

"He walks soft and carries a big stick," said Toaster.

"You mean the shotgun?"

"That's more than a shotgun, Graham. Up close, there's nothing deadlier. I'd like to know where he got it."

"Rare, are they?"

Toaster turned to look across the back of the seat and down at the carrier bag. "Over here they're invisible. Rare and expensive. It must have cost the price of a small car. They're illegal, see. So you can't nick them from a gun club or a farmer. Although the law have them. They're illegal against birds, grouse and pheasants. But God help the pregnant old tart who stumbles into a siege or an ambush one dark night. They won't be illegal against her. They'll tell the coroner she farted and he'll be most understanding."

"Why are they so special?"

Toaster moved his head. "Take a look at the bastard. See how neat and compact it is. Powerful, reliable,

76

accurate. And you can afford to miss seven times. If you're near enough, with a twelve-gauge, that's almost impossible."

Beasley looked down at the gun. "It's sort of asking you to touch it, isn't it? What'll he do with it afterwards? The way he was talking you'd think he was going to sling it into the canal."

"I doubt it," said Toaster. "There's no rifling, see. They won't have a bullet looking for a barrel. They'll just have a lot of metal and they won't know where it came from. Tom's just putting the frighteners on us."

"You've got no respect for science, Toaster."

Toaster smiled. "We'll see." He tapped his index finger against his temple. "Whatever he does, he'll do it right."

"Here he is."

Goff moved up along the side of the van and tapped on the window. Toaster stretched across the seat to release the door catch.

Goff swung into the van and pushed the door shut. "All quiet?"

"Nothing," said Toaster.

"Good," said Goff. His left hand fell over the back of the seat to touch the carrier bag. "It all looks jake to me. There was an old tramp dossing behind us. I roused him up but we'll make sure he's gone when we check the other car."

"It looks good, Tom?"

"It does, Toaster. You've got a fine eye. Provided they don't all come out together, we ought to take them before they get into the Ford. We'll move near to give us more time."

"What do you mean, if they don't all come out together?" said Toaster. "They went in four together, they're very likely to come out four together."

"Ease down, Toaster," said Goff. "Four I can handle. I meant if the other three come out with them. They're all law, you said. So it's not unlikely. Seven could be messy. If it's seven, we leave it. If it's four, we'll take them."

"And what if it's five or six?" said Toaster.

"If it's more than four, we'll leave it alone."

"How do you plan to do it?" said Beasley.

"Graham's a bit disappointed at the lack of diagrams and stopwatches," said Toaster. "He wanted meticulous planning."

"Leave it out, Toaster," said Beasley.

Goff looked across Toaster at Beasley. "When the business is bodies, it's best to be loose and ready for anything. People aren't predictable. We might need to improvise. So the sketchier the better."

"You mean no plan at all? Just wait and blast?"

"No, no," said Goff, "we'll have an outline. I'll show you."

Goff jiggled the gear stick and started the engine. He drove, without lights, across the car park and stopped thirty yards behind the Ford. He turned off the key and lifted the handbrake.

Toaster looked behind him. "This'll make it a fair old dash if we're going out the back," he said.

"We'll stroll," said Goff. "There'll be no one keen to catch us."

"That's true."

"Now," said Goff. "I'll be in your seat, Graham. As soon as they've come far enough I'll get out that door and show them the gun."

"What do you mean, far enough?"

"So they can't run back inside. Once they're in the lamplight, they're ours. These are all trained men, they should know how to react to firearms. They should be docile. But they'll have drink aboard so we can't be sure. If they do it by the book, I'll rack them up against their own car. Then we'll lift their valuables. I want you to do that, Toaster."

"Sure, but why?"

"Just to muddy up the water. Maybe they'll think it's a mugging that went sour. Take wallets, money, keys. Once you've stepped clear I'm going to blow the legs off Swakely and Kilbride."

"What?" said Toaster.

"You heard."

"For fuck's sake, why?"

"It's a gesture. It's needed. To let them know who we are."

Toaster rubbed his hands up and down his face. "That's stupid, Tom, that's fucking stupid. If the shock don't kill them outright, it'll certainly kill their interest in who fired it. And what sort of a mugger would do a thing like that?"

Goff kissed his teeth and looked past Toaster to the pale-faced Beasley. "Never mind then. Let me see your helmets."

Toaster and Beasley unfurled the rims of their cloth caps. The holes for eyes and mouth were trimmed with leather borders. The masks clung tight to their faces and ended just below the chin.

"They're fine," said Goff.

"Hot and itchy," said Toaster. He rolled the helmet back into a rim around his forehead. "I prefer the Mickey Mouse jobs."

"What about the other two?" said Beasley. He'd taken off his cap and re-set it in his lap before stretching it across the top of his head.

"What other two?" said Goff.

"The two with Swakely and Kilbride."

"They'll be no problem," said Goff.

"Well, I mean, one of them probably isn't even a cricketer."

"But law, though, definitely law?"

"I suppose."

"You know what we said. Policemen make good witnesses, Graham. There's going to be no witnesses."

"Okay, okay," said Beasley. "I just thought they'd all be cricketers."

"It's better in a way," said Goff.

"Why?"

"Widens the motive."

Beasley adjusted his cap, turning away from Goff. "There's going to be one hell of a fuss," he said. "Four copper corpses. The papers are going to need a new size of type."

Goff leant across Toaster and gripped Beasley by the upper arm. "What's wrong with you, Graham? We've been through all this."

"I know, I know."

Goff tugged Beasley towards him. "They'll check everything, Graham. Every case, every file, every rumour. They're going to want to talk to you. They're going to want to talk to hundreds. But you're ready for them, aren't you?"

"I'm ready. You know I'm ready."

"I'm not thinking about myself, Graham. I'll be long gone. You think about yourself and you think about Toaster. You stay staunch and they'll move on to someone else. You start to blub and the man who holds your hand will be putting ink on the tips of your fingers."

Beasley levered his arm free of Goff's grip. "As you said, we've been through all this."

"Just so you remember it," said Goff. "You can go home now, Graham, right this minute. I told you before you're not needed. None of us will think the worse of you for changing your mind. But they're still going to want to talk to you."

Toaster rested both hands on the dashboard, dividing Goff from Beasley. "Leave him alone, Tom," he said. "Graham's not going to blub. He's a lot tougher than he looks. I'm more concerned about the other problem."

"What problem?"

"Your problem. This cowboy shit about shooting off their legs."

"I said forget it."

"Yeah," said Toaster. "But have you forgotten it?" He held up a gloved hand and ticked off the fingers. "One for Swakely's legs. One for Kilbride's legs. One for goodnight Swakely. One for goodnight Kilbride. One for the first witness. One for the second witness. That makes six. You said it was an eight-shot magazine, Tom. If you

80

let six go and suddenly we're embarrassed, where are we going to be, Thomas?"

"Up to our eyeballs in blood," said Beasley.

"You shut up, Graham," said Toaster.

"Stop worrying, Toaster," said Goff. "I said there'd be no problems."

Toaster smiled at him and turned towards the windscreen. He spread his arms, embracing the car park. "Then this'll do nicely."

"It will if we're careful," said Goff. "Let's go and check that spare motor."

"Suits me," said Toaster.

"Hey up," said Beasley. "The late, late trade."

A white saloon car, headlights bouncing, turned into the car park and reversed up to the warehouse wall. The engine stopped and the main beam winked into sidelights. Five men got out of the car and moved towards the club. The last two men were handcuffed together.

"Surely they're not nicked?" said Beasley.

"No, they're all law," said Toaster. "Just playing about. Probably lost the key. I told you it was a den of blue, Tom."

"So you did. There'll be a round dozen in there now."

"They've left their lights on," said Beasley.

"They looked well oiled," said Toaster. He pushed against Goff with his shoulder. "You want to see the other car?"

"What?" said Goff, staring through the windscreen.

"You wanted to check the spare wheels."

"I did, I did. But give them a chance to settle, Toaster. One of them might come back for his brains."

Toaster sat straight in his seat, pulling his elbows into his waist, clenching his fists, pushing his shoulders back. "I hope they've lost those keys forever," he said.

Beasley smiled. "With any luck they'll have to get the fire brigade to cut them loose."

"There's something nasty about cuffs," said Goff.

Goff

Goff opened his eyes and moved his neck from side to side. His hand was shackled to the foot-rest. He lay stretched out on the floor at a right angle to the bar. To his left, three policemen were drinking at the table near the toilet. To his right sat Beasley, his legs tucked under him, Toaster's head in his lap. Beasley's left hand only was shackled to the foot-rest. In his right hand he held a blood-soaked rag which he dabbed at Toaster's ear.

"How he is?" said Goff.

"I dunno. Bad. Shock or something. What about yourself?"

"What happened?"

"The big sergeant – Swakely – he hit you for no reason. Whack, whack, whack with the billiard cue. That got Toaster going and the Oaf tore out his ear-ring."

"I saw that. I meant afterwards."

"Well, when you hit the Oaf, they carried him next door and chained us up. Told me to clean up Toaster. Refused a doctor. You took a terrible couple of smacks. How do you feel?"

"Like a plane crash. How long was I out?"

"Half an hour. Three quarters."

"And Toaster?"

"He opens his eyes now and then but he don't say nothing. Shock or something. Like I said."

"Turn his head this way."

Beasley shifted his body and lifted Toaster's head towards Goff.

"He doesn't look good," said Goff. "Has the bleeding stopped?"

"Yeah. Except he moves every now and then and it starts again."

"Animals," said Goff.

"I warned you."

"So you did. How's that Inspector doing?"

"Suffering."

"Good."

"You gave him two beauties. I've never seen anyone change colour so quick. They've taken him up to the clinic."

"They're keeping us here until he recovers, are they?"

Beasley looked towards the policeman's table. "Not really. They're waiting for the main nick to fill up. They're still arresting people from the march. As soon as King Street is full they start dispersing prisoners all around the place. They want to take us to the Vale."

"Yeah?"

"You've heard of it?"

"I've been a long time abroad, Graham. What's so special about it?"

"It's a little out-of-the-way nick. Condemned years ago and opened up again when they started the extension at King Street. It's where they hide you away from your brief or the Press. Things like that."

"Like beating the shit out of you?"

"So they say."

"That figures. But why the delay? Why aren't we there already?"

Beasley dipped his mouth close to Goff's ear. "The Oaf's got no pull. He's bad news everywhere. If they took us to the Vale before King Street was full, there might be questions. They might lose us. They don't want that. They're too keen. You made him look a lemon."

Goff moved his head from between his outstretched arms and wriggled into a sitting position, leaning his shoulder against the bar. "What about yourself, Graham. Are you hurt? Did you pitch in?"

"No. I was over by the wall. Anything I could have done, I was scared to do. This is not my game, Mr Goff.

There were at least seven of them. I know because I counted fourteen. No fighter, no hero, no balls. That's me."

"You probably did right."

"I'm still going to get a kicking though, ain't I?"

"Try not to worry. It'll be me he wants."

"These are not very discriminating people, Mr Goff."

"I suppose not."

"Anything that looks alive is likely to get a pasting."

"That doesn't have to be true, Graham."

Beasley began rocking backwards and forwards on his haunches, pressing Toaster's head into his stomach. "The only fighting I ever do is on the tube. I'm the elbow champion of the Circle Line, the armrest king of the underground. Never give an inch, never swallow a liberty. There's hundreds, thousands who'd rather stand than sit next to me. I can work some pushy sod into the next carriage when my dander's up. They're all at it, you know. Vicious young secretaries, aggressive old grandads, bullies in bowlers. And all done in silence. Never any eye contact, never mind complaints. A seasoned campaigner like me can unroll a toffee or turn his paper without ever moving the elbows."

"A very potent weapon, the elbow," said Goff.

Beasley closed his eyes and dropped his head. "Sorry about that."

"You're bearing up well, son. Have you had a chance to use that famous ear on this lot?"

Beasley expelled a heavy breath of air. "Nothing much. They were having a bit of a giggle about what you did to the Oaf. And there was some talk about paying you off in here. But the sergeant put a stop to that."

"Grace before their meal, is it?"

Beasley shrugged and brushed the cloth across Toaster's forehead.

Goff looked towards the policemen and raised his voice. "Hey."

They all turned towards him. "Back with us, eh?" said the nearest. "Get the sergeant, Benny."

"Who the fuck do you think you are, Davis? Get him yourself."

Davis stood up and sighed. "The burdens of command." He walked to the counter flap, leant through and shouted into the public bar, "Sergeant. You there, sarge?"

Sergeant Swakely, coat unbuttoned, a drink in his hand, came through into the lounge. "What now?"

"The gorilla's awake."

Swakely stretched across the counter to look down at Goff. "Already?"

"I want to talk to you," said Goff.

"Is that so?" said Swakely. He lifted the flap and entered the saloon, walking around to stand in front of Goff. "You've made a good recovery. I wouldn't have advised it though."

"Never mind about me. The boy looks bad."

"Big deal."

"It might be if he dies."

"Who said anything about dying? Drama. He's only lost a bit of blood."

"He's a diabetic," said Goff. "And he's lost a lot of blood. You're in charge now, sergeant. If he dies it'll all be down to you refusing medical help."

The sergeant crouched over Toaster. He tipped a portion of his drink into Toaster's mouth. "Diabetic? What's that got to do with anything? Means he can't take sugar."

"Don't show your ignorance," said Goff. "He was going home for an injection just as you arrived. He needs insulin."

Swakely stood up and shook his head. He turned to Davis. "What do you think, Ron?"

Davis said, "He looks all right to me. Sweet."

Goff looked up at Davis. "What does he know about medicine?"

"He's taken the course," said the sergeant. "Ain't you, Ron?"

"I'm practically a surgeon," said Davis.

Goff jerked his head at Davis and spoke to the sergeant. "I reckon he's the type who nips into the morgue to cool his tool."

Davis plunged between the sergeant and Goff, reaching for Goff's throat. Goff's left leg flashed a kick at him. Davis fell backwards. As he tried to rise, his leg quivered and he collapsed again. The sergeant restrained him.

"Next time I'll snap the kneecap," said Goff.

The sergeant helped Davis stand. Davis pointed his index finger at Goff. "When W.G.'s finished with you, I'm going to start. I'm going to strip the skin off your cock in tiny slivers and ram them up your arse with a five-speed drill."

"There you are," said Goff to the sergeant. "I told you he was a pervert."

Swakely pushed Davis back towards his table and turned to Goff. "Knock it off, you. You're in enough shit."

"Not as much as you'll be in if the lad dies."

"Relax, for God's sake. We'll be off to the station in a minute. We'll get someone to look at him there."

"Hey, sarge, sarge," Kilbride shouted from behind the bar.

"What?"

Kilbride gestured at the sergeant to join him.

Swakely looked down at Goff. "Wait here," he said and laughed, a high, squeaking intake of breath.

"If I had a laugh like that I wouldn't be so easily amused," said Goff.

Swakely laughed again and walked towards Kilbride. They began speaking and the other three policemen gathered at the counter flap. Goff heard Swakely say, "We can't go that far." Swakely and Kilbride returned to the public bar. The three policemen re-seated themselves at the table.

"What was all that about?" Goff said to Beasley.

Beasley shrugged. "I wasn't listening."

"That's ace," said Goff.

"These are real bad people, Mr Goff. I don't think

you realize that. I mean, goading them and taking the piss. You're chancing it."

"Is that what you think?"

"Just thought I'd clue you in, that's all."

"I was in Kampala with Idi Amin and all I can remember is that they served the whiskey in Coca-Cola bottles."

"Yeah? Very interesting. But, if you don't mind me saying so, so what?"

"There was some real bad people there then, Graham. It's just that they're easy to forget."

"You think so? You think Toaster's going to forget? For the rest of his life, every time he fingers his ear-lobe he's – hold up, they're coming back."

Swakely, followed by Kilbride and two other policemen, filed through the flap. Swakely was carrying a truncheon and had buttoned up his coat.

"Right, you lot," Swakely said to the officers at the table. "Let's see some action. Get the gypsy into the van. And gently. We don't want pools of blood smearing all the gear. One of you get some newspapers down first, just in case. You, Sullivan."

Two of the policemen lifted Toaster by the legs and shoulders. A third supported his head and back.

"Save your dirty looks for later," Swakely said to Goff. "He's going straight to hospital."

"This way," said Kilbride, holding open the toilet door. "We'll have to take him through the public."

Swakely watched his officers manoeuvre Toaster through the door and turned back to Goff and Beasley, smiling, looking from one to the other, smacking the truncheon into the palm of his left hand.

"That's a lovely pose, sergeant," said Goff. "Did you work it out yourself? Doesn't he look tough, Graham?"

Kilbride came up to stand beside the sergeant.

"Do the shrimp first," said Swakely. "The South African cuff."

Kilbride crouched on one knee to release Beasley's handcuff from the foot-rest. "Stand up," he told him.

"Now put your hands between your legs. No, one hand through the back. That's it."

With his hands shackled around his thigh, Beasley was unable to stand upright.

"Get him in the van," said Swakely. "No. Hold it a minute." He looked down at Goff. "What's your name, big boy?"

Goff smiled at him.

Swakely clicked his tongue. "Why do I always get a smartarse?" He turned to Beasley. "What's his name?"

Beasley shuffled sideways. "I don't know. Honest. I only met him today. Just here. In this pub."

Swakely beat a rapid tattoo with his truncheon on Beasley's stooped head. Beasley jerked away from the blows and almost fell.

"Now don't fuck about," said Swakely. "What's his name?"

"I'm telling you the truth," shouted Beasley. "Honest to God. I only met him today. His first name's Tom, I think. That's all I know."

"Tom, eh?" said Swakely. "Well, that'll do for now." He tapped Beasley on the skull again. "Nice tone that. Might well finish that march later. All right, get him out."

Beasley staggered sideways and shuffled out through the toilet door, a policeman shoving at his shoulder.

Davis and one of the officers who had removed Toaster appeared behind the bar.

"Davis, Swan," said Swakely. "Get around here."

The two officers came through the counter flap.

"All right out there?" said the sergeant.

"He is breathing and he ain't bleeding," said Davis.

"Did you get that paper down?"

"No paper. We tore up some crisp cartons. It'll be all right."

"Quiet out there, is it? No gawpers?"

"Lovely."

"Let's get it finished then."

Swakely moved to stand just beyond Goff's feet, both

fists tight around the truncheon. "Tom, is it? Tom. Good old-fashioned name. I've been thinking about you, Tom. You know what we call toms, don't you? Give one of them a slap and she's yours forever. Well, a short time, anyway." He swayed forward and squeaked into laughter. "But you, Tom, you're a different number altogether. I gave you a taste of that billiard cue and I wasn't being gentle. But did that keep you quiet? Nooooa. A few minutes later you jump up and take a sneaky dig at the guv'nor. So then old Swanny here, he gives you a bit of stick and he assures me he held nothing back. And does that keep you quiet? Nooooa. Incredible. Half an hour later you're rabbitting away ten to the dozen and then you've got the gall to assault a second officer. And you're full of lip, too. Offensive lip. Alluding to Mr Davis here as a pervert. When you should be feeling sick, sore and sorry for yourself. Humble's what we expected but humble ain't what we got. Resilient. That's what you are, Tom. Resilient. And probably a psychopath, too, the way you keep attacking us guardians of the peace." He paused, nodding his head and running his left hand up and down the truncheon. "So what I want to know, Tom, what I want to know is whether you're going to come quietly, as we say, or whether I need to knock some sense into you, some humility. With this."

He whipped the truncheon shuddering down onto the bar just above Goff's head. From below, Goff could see a jagged arc of splinters quivering on the bruised edge of the bar.

"I'll bet you say that to all the girls," said Goff.

Swakely smiled, looking around at the other officers. "See what I mean. Resilient. The man's resilient." He stared down at Goff. "But we've no time for jokes, Thomas. So how do you want it? Hard or easy, it's entirely up to you."

Goff ran his eyes around the semi-circle of policemen. "Bad odds tied up this way." He tugged his hands against the shackles. "All right, sergeant, I'll come like a lamb if you promise not to laugh again."

Swakely cupped his left hand to his mouth. "Is it all right if I smother the mirth like this, Tom? Giggle behind the palm. That won't upset you, will it?"

Goff gestured with his head towards the toilet. "But I'm not going out handcuffed that way, like that poor sod, shuffling along like a hunchback who's lost a fifty-pound note. I'll give you no trouble otherwise."

"Aah," said Swakely, placing the truncheon on the back of his neck and using it as a brace to stretch his shoulders. "You want to go out with dignity, do you, Tom? Walking tall and straight. But no can do. We don't want you feeling proud and strong, Tom. You can understand that. You've been naughty, Thomas. You've upset us. And it's not in our natures to be kind, to forgive and forget. So let's not engage in a little battle of wills. Accept the inevitable, Thomas. You go out like a crab. We'll all feel safer that way. And a little superior, too, I won't deny that. So, it's no deals. You've got a straight choice. Go out like a crab. Or go out like a bruised crab. Now, what do you say?'

Goff coughed, cleared his throat, hawking spittle into his mouth. He looked right and left along the foot-rest. "There's no spittoon in this bar. Do you mind bending down a bit, sergeant, and opening that big gob of yours?"

Swakely slashed down with the truncheon, hitting Goff on the shoulder and dancing clear as Goff's feet whirled up at him. Kilbride threw himself across Goff's thighs, pinning his legs to the floor. Goff dropped his head and began to work his teeth through the collar of Kilbride's uniform and into his neck. Kilbride screamed. Goff's head was snapped away by another truncheon blow. Swan took a handful of his hair and forced his head back against the foot-rest. Davis splayed his legs apart.

Kilbride stood up, fingering his collar, his eyes jumping. "The bastard tried to bite my head off. He really did. Look at this. Fuck me, he is King Kong. He's a fucking crazy, I'm telling you, he's a fucking crazy." He dropped his right knee into Goff's ribs and positioned himself for a head-butt.

Swakely stiff-armed Kilbride away. "Now, now, Will, cool down. You don't want to spoil him for W.G. Get those cuffs off the rail."

"They're Swanny's," said Kilbride.

"Give him room then," said Swakely.

"Here," said Swan. "Somebody cop his barnet. I don't want to lose any fingers."

"It's safer on a picket line," said Kilbride.

With help from Swakely, Davis and Kilbride, Swan removed the handcuffs from the foot-rest. Swakely forced Goff's right arm behind his back and down to his thigh. Swan levered the left arm into position and the locks were set.

"Right, get him up," said Swakely

Goff was hauled onto his feet, his back bent, head lolling against his left arm. Swan swung him towards the toilet door and Goff struck with his feet. Swan fell. Swakely swung his truncheon and Goff collapsed on Swan.

"Fucking hell," said Davis.

Kilbride kicked at Goff and pulled Swan clear. "Bastard."

"We'll have to cuff his feet," said Davis.

"Then how the fuck's he going to walk?"

"He's not, is he?"

"You all right, mate?" said Kilbride, rubbing at Swan's leg.

"I'm fine. Thanks, Will. Just get me up."

Kilbride looped Swan's arm around his neck and steered him to the table near the toilets.

"You're right, the bastard's not going to walk," said Swakely. "If we had the time I'd teach him to bounce out of here on his head. But we haven't. So cuff his feet and we'll lug him. At least, you lot will. I'll go and square the landlord."

Kilbride and Davis dragged Goff through the men's toilet and then through the public-bar doors. Swan limped behind them.

At the police van, Swan was needed to lift Goff,

bleeding from a cut on the bridge of his nose, into the aisles between the seats. Davis climbed into the van behind him and levered Goff under a double seat with his feet. Toaster was lying on a bed of cardboard at the front. Beasley was sitting opposite him.

One of the policemen already in the van said to Davis, "More trouble?"

"He stuck one on Swanny."

"How's Toaster?" Goff called to Beasley.

"The same."

"Shut up, you," Davis said to Beasley. "And you," he added, kicking at Goff.

Kilbride climbed into the driving seat and started the engine. Sullivan entered the van through the rear door and locked it behind him. Swakely was the last to enter, taking the front passenger seat.

"We couldn't have timed it better," said Swakely. "Straight to the Vale once you've dropped the gypsy, Will. You stay with him at the hospital, Swanny. Have them look at your leg."

"It's only bruised," said Swan.

"Somebody's got to stay at the hospital."

"I'm owed."

"Don't worry," said Swakely. "All debts will be more than settled."

"What about W.G.?" said Kilbride.

"He's meeting us at the Vale."

Swakely dipped his head beneath the seats. "You all right down there, Thomas? Not hurt your dignity or anything, have we?"

"The only thing you offend, sergeant, is my sense of smell."

"Spunky, ain't he?" said Kilbride.

Swakely straightened up and looked at him. "You waiting for promotion?"

Kilbride laughed and engaged the gears.

Beasley, guided by Davis, took the steps one at a time. Davis released him at the entrance and Beasley overbalanced, striking his head against the door.

"That's malicious damage, you clumsy bugger," said Davis. He opened the door and swung Beasley inside.

Swakely, Kilbride and Evans carried Goff in behind them.

"Straight through," said Swakely. "Straight to the charge room."

Davis opened a side door facing the information counter and pushed Beasley into a green-walled corridor. Beasley stumbled against the wall, smearing the condensation. At the end of the corridor was a large room bisected by a wooden counter. Beasley was pushed onto a bench and Goff was dropped at his feet.

Behind the counter a sergeant with a purple birthmark on his left cheek said, "What's all this?"

Swakely stepped up to the counter and held out his hand. "Arthur Swakely. You must be Sergeant Overland."

The sergeant shook hands. "That's right. Peter Overland."

Swakely looked back at Goff and Beasley. "You're taking some of the demo overflow, aren't you?"

"Are they full already?" said Overland. He half-turned and shouted, "Horace. Hey, Horace."

"Oh, Jesus," said Swakely.

"What's wrong?" said Overland.

"It's nothing. Is the wine cellar free?"

"Free? It's practically floating," laughed Overland.

"I'd like to book it for these two."

"You're kidding."

Swakely pointed at Goff. "You see that slab of meat? He beat the shit out of our guv'nor."

"I don't know," said Overland.

"I don't think you heard me right," said Swakely.

Behind Overland, a man in shirtsleeves, dry-washing his face with both hands, emerged from a door marked *Interview Room One*. He looked at the group on the far side of the counter and said, "Good grief, the cricketers. What have you caught this time?"

"Constable Horace Lyons," said Swakely. "Still moonlighting, by the cracks in his eyes. Tut, tut. Kipping in the middle of your shift, Horace? Back on the mini-cabs, are you?"

Lyons took a jacket from the back of a chair and put it on. "Where's the Oaf?"

"Watch your lip, Horace," said Swakely.

"I watch everything while you're around, Arthur. Mostly my wallet. Where is he? Gone to buy a blow-torch?"

Swakely looked at the ceiling, smiled at Overland and shook his head at Lyons. "Do you ever wonder why you've been a P C for thirty years, Horace?"

Lyons buttoned his jacket and straightened his tie. "No, Arthur, I've never wondered, I've always known."

Swakely waited and then said to Overland, "I don't mind being his dummy. Go on, Horace, tell us why then."

Lyons picked at his nose with his thumb and moved up alongside Overland. "Faulty vision. I've never been able to tell the difference between a prick and a superior officer. A bag of shit and a bag of shit with stripes is still a bag of shit. Isn't that right, Will?"

Davis laughed.

Kilbride said, "Leave me out of this, Horace."

Swakely looked at Davis. "When you're his age, it won't be so funny."

Lyons moved along the counter for a closer look at

Goff and Beasley. "You'll get your ears warmed for cuffing them like that," he said to Swakely.

"Why do you love to stir it up?" said Swakely. "My ears can look after themselves." He turned to Overland. "What about the cellar?"

Lyons said, "What about the cellar?"

"I'm not asking the monkey."

Lyons said to Overland, "Don't let him bullshit you, Peter."

"He says King Street's full," said Overland.

"He would, wouldn't he."

"It's easy to check," said Swakely.

"It's even easier to keep you out of here," said Lyons. "We're not complete cunts, Arthur."

Swakely moved closer to the counter, dropping his voice. "It's an assault on an officer, Horace."

Lyons probed his right ear, examined an extricated piece of wax and flicked it away from under his fingernail. "Mmm." He looked at Goff and Beasley again. "Well, it can't be one of you lot because these two are still alive as far as I can see."

"It was on W.G. himself," said Swakely.

"Really? Lurking about in the gents, was he?"

"It was a serious assault, Horace. He couldn't move for an hour."

"He'll piss blood for a week," said Kilbride.

Swakely swung away from the counter to face Kilbride. "You've said that once and I didn't like it much then."

"Where's the Oaf now?" said Lyons.

"He'll be along in a while."

"To pay his respects?"

"What else?"

Lyons scratched his hair with both hands. "Yeah, yeah, all right. I'll check with King Street first, though. And get them cuffed up right, Arthur, or it goes in the report." He walked towards the door at the back of the room.

"Will I give them the cellar?" Overland called.

Lyons opened the door and turned. "Let me check first, Peter. Don't let them near anything detachable. And I'm not talking about the prisoners." He stretched his mouth at Swakely and left the room.

"Bloody hell," said Kilbride.

"He gave you some stick, sarge," said Davis.

"That's his style," said Swakely. "Says his prayers with a pint of beer in his hand. And looks down, not up." He moved across to Goff and Beasley. "All right, get the cuffs changed and sit them both on the bench. Can I use the phone, Peter?"

"As long as it's not Australia."

"Local clinic."

Overland lifted the flap to let Swakely through. He pointed to a white telephone on one of the desks. "Direct line there."

Evans, with Davis standing guard, released Beasley and re-cuffed his hands behind his back.

"Put him in the corner," said Kilbride, waving his truncheon at the end of the bench. He jabbed the truncheon into Goff's shoulder. "We're cuffing you up neat and orderly as prescribed by the Home Office, big boy. So behave yourself this time."

"Get on with it," said Goff.

Evans and Davis took the cuffs from Goff's feet and re-set the others behind his back.

"There's nothing wrong with nice and tight," Kilbride said to Davis.

"You're a disgrace to your race, Kilbride," said Goff.

Kilbride bent over until his face was close to Goff's. "And how do you know my name? If you want to make a complaint it's my number you'll be wanting." He turned his shoulder towards Goff. "Take a good gander."

"Oh, I've got your number, son. Don't you worry about that."

"You flash bastard," said Kilbride, holding the truncheon up to Goff's mouth. "I've got a good mind to make you eat this."

"That's enough," said Overland.

"Yeah, knock it off," called Swakely, sitting on the desk with a phone in his hand. "W.G. will be here in about twenty minutes. You can play lollipops then. And you can warn him about his urine, Will." He dialled a number and hung up. "My missus must be on the game."

Overland lifted the flap to allow Swakely back to the other side of the counter. "What about the charges, sergeant?"

"Ah, now," said Swakely, "let me sort that out." He pointed at Goff. "The hulk first." He held up his left hand and began to pick off the fingers. "Three assaults on a police officer on three separate occasions. Obstruction. Breach of the peace. Criminal damage to a billiard cue. What have I missed, Will?"

"Attempted cannibalism."

Swakely squeaked into laughter. "We'll save that. The other one? I'm not sure. We'll have to wait for W.G. Drunk and disorderly for now. Maybe accessory later. Did he resist arrest, Will?"

Kilbride stepped up in front of Beasley. "Have you got any form, Graham?"

"What do you mean?" said Beasley.

"Oh, dear, I think he did resist arrest," said Kilbride. "Probably assaulted me too. Not quite sure yet. Can't hear what he's saying. Have you got any form?"

"Tell him how you won the Derby last year," said Goff.

"You," said Kilbride, pointing his truncheon at Goff. "You, I can taste you already. I just can't wait to have you."

Goff pursed his lips in a kiss.

"Very tense in here," said Lyons, massaging his left armpit as he came up behind Overland.

"You're back just in time to see how well my lads withstand provocation," said Swakely.

"What's the position?" Overland said to Lyons.

"We can book 'em here."

"You've got to have more faith, Horace," said Swakely.

Lyons signalled Swakely to approach him. "Arthur, you dropped a young lad off at the hospital?"

"That's right."

"Better be prepared for some questions then. He's not too well."

"He only cut his ear."

Lyons tapped his left breast. "Dodgy ticker."

"He's just a kid."

"The heart has no rules, Arthur. You should know that."

"What the hell does that mean?"

"Come, come, Arthur, you surely don't want details. And you surrounded by youth."

"Arseholes to that crap."

"Not now, for God's sake," said Overland. "Let's get them charged."

"I'll have a word with you later, Horace," said Swakely.

"I'm sure you will, Arthur, but I'm a bit short myself."

"What a comedian."

"Get them up here," Overland said to Kilbride.

Goff and Beasley were positioned in front of the counter facing Overland and Lyons.

"What's wrong with the kid?" Goff said to Lyons.

"Friend of yours, is he?"

"That's right."

"Well, he's got a bad heart. There's complications."

"What sort of complications?"

"That's all I know. If I hear anything else, I'll pass it on."

"Thanks."

"Quite ready now?" Overland said to Goff.

"Get on with it," said Goff.

Overland looked at Swakely. "Drunk and disorderly, you said?"

"Yeah, the little one."

Overland opened the charge book and said to Beasley, "Name and address?"

"Graham Beasley, one hundred and thirty four Addison Road."

"Just up the road?"

"Yes."

"Got a middle name?"

"No."

Overland wrote in the book. "Date of birth."

"August seventh, nineteen fifty-nine."

Kilbride tore a page from his notebook and laid it on the counter in front of Overland. He copied details into the book.

"All right, Graham," said Overland. "You're charged with being drunk and disorderly at The Castle public house, Dean Street, at 3.10 pm, today, February 23rd. You do not have to say anything but anything you do say may be taken down and used in evidence against you. Do you understand?"

"Yes."

Swakely slapped his hand on the counter. "What were you doing at Wood Green?" he said to Overland.

"Traffic analysis. Why?"

"You don't caution drunks. Not much point, is there? If they're drunk."

Lyons touched Overland's elbow. "Sergeant Overland has his doubts about this man's level of intoxication," he said. "He was asking as a means of gauging the prisoner's response."

"Bollocks," said Swakely.

"You're acting very strangely for a man who's wanting a favour, Arthur," said Lyons.

Swakely laughed. "Ain't I just. Sorry about that, Peter. Didn't realize you were so thorough."

Overland said to Beasley, "Well, do you want to say anything?"

"No."

"There," said Kilbride. "I knew he had form."

"Keep quiet," said Overland.

"What about bail?" said Beasley.

"We'll check your address out first and then we'll see. You can't leave until you've sobered up. And you may be wanted for questioning on another matter. All right, just move down there and turn your pockets out."

Davis took Beasley by the elbow and guided him further down the counter. Davis removed the handcuffs and Beasley began to empty his pockets in front of Lyons who was making a list of his possessions.

Overland said to Goff, "Name and address?"

"I want a solicitor."

"You have to be charged first."

"I want a solicitor."

"I must warn you that failure to supply your name and address is in itself another offence."

"I want a solicitor."

"Such an attitude is not in your own best interests."

"I want a solicitor."

"Very well. Turn out your pockets, please."

"If I could turn out my pockets chained like this I'd be on the stage."

Overland nodded to Kilbride. "Okay, let's have his possessions."

Kilbride went through Goff's pockets and placed money, two handkerchiefs, a comb, a pair of glasses in a leather sheath, a bunch of keys and a flask on the counter.

"There must be more," said Overland, unscrewing the top of the flask and sniffing the contents.

Kilbride went through Goff's pockets again, checking seams and linings, dipping into his socks. "That's it."

"No wallet?" Overland said to Goff.

"What do I want a wallet for? I know who I am."

"Credit cards?"

"I use money."

"So I see." Overland counted the money. "One hundred and eighty-seven pounds and seventy-three pence. That's rather a lot of money."

"Do you think so?"

"Where did you get it?"

"I want a solicitor."

Overland picked up the bunch of keys. "We'll soon find your car, you know. You might as well co-operate."

Goff leaned towards Overland and jerked his head

behind him. "These bastards brought me in here so they can kick the shit out of me. What sort of co-operation did you have in mind?"

Overland looked down the counter. "Horace."

Lyons moved up beside him. "Yeah, I've been listening." He examined the money and the keys. He put his finger in his ear and strummed his wrist. "This won't do you any good," he said to Goff.

"The only thing you should put in your ear is your elbow," said Goff.

Lyons smiled and removed his finger from his ear. He flicked at the top of his finger with his thumb. "We'll just have to keep you here until we find out who you are. Have you any objections to being fingerprinted?"

Swakely said, "For Pete's sake, Horace."

"Yes, I think I have," said Goff.

"Then we'll just take you into court tomorrow and get the magistrate to order you to comply. We'll use force if necessary. And if that doesn't tell us who you are, we'll try something else. One thing's for certain. You won't get out of here until we're sure of who you are."

"That's right," said Overland.

Lyons turned the charge book towards himself.

"Here," said Swakely, handing Lyons his notebook.

Lyons read the book and looked up at Goff. "These are serious charges."

"And that's just for starters," said Swakely.

Goff smiled. "All the more reason to have a solicitor."

"Mmm. Peter," said Lyons. He pulled Overland away from the counter to one of the desks.

"What sort of cunt's stunt do you think this is?" Swakely said to Goff. He walked around Goff to Beasley. "You, you little turd. What's his name and address?"

"I told you already. I only met him today."

"Now I'm sure he assaulted me," said Kilbride.

Overland returned to the counter. "Just a minute."

Lyons opened the door at the back of the room and

shouted, "Samuels, Gordon. Bring Parkinson as well. He's upstairs."

"Just for the record, I'll ask you again for your name and address," Overland said to Goff.

"I want a solicitor."

"Then you will be kept here until we have established your identity to our satisfaction."

Three policemen had joined Lyons at the back of the room. He led them up to the counter and opened the flap to allow them through. They took up positions behind Goff and Beasley. Lyons remained on the other side.

"Why all the extra artillery, Horace?" said Swakely.

"Take off his cuffs so that he can sign for his possessions," said Lyons.

Swakely nodded at Kilbride who unlocked Goff's handcuffs.

Overland turned a sheet of paper towards Goff and laid a pen on top of it. "Check it and sign."

Overland walked back to the nearest desk and began to search through one of the drawers. Lyons checked off Beasley's possessions and told him where to sign.

Goff read the list, signed and threw the pen on the counter. Overland left the desk and picked up the list. He passed it to Lyons.

"What's he signed?" said Swakely.

"An X," said Overland.

"He's a piss-taker," said Davis.

"Aren't we all?" Goff said to Lyons.

Lyons shrugged. "You're playing a silly game, old chum." He came through the counter flap and approached Goff. "Excuse me." He opened Goff's top coat and looked at the inside pocket. He did the same with the jacket of the suit. "Good material. You'll have to leave the tie on the counter."

"Not my boots?"

"We only worry about the laces. It's not such a joke, you know."

Goff draped his tie across the counter. "What were you looking for?" he said to Lyons.

"Labels. I don't know about the coat but that's a handmade suit. No labels, no wallet. There's something funny about you."

"I'm not an advertising board."

"No. But what are you?"

"I'm a man who wants a solicitor."

"It's a doctor you're going to need," said Kilbride.

"Shut up, Will," said Lyons. "Right, Mr X. These officers will take you to a cell while further inquiries are made."

"The cellar, Horace," said Swakely.

Lyons stepped aside and signalled to Samuels who was standing behind Goff. Samuels reached forward and gripped Goff's upper right arm.

Goff twisted free and turned to face him. "I'm not a blind man."

Lyons said, "Let him alone as long as he goes quietly, Bob."

"You're a real spoilsport, Horace."

"I told you to shut up, Kilbride."

"Yeah, put a sock in it, Will," said Swakely.

"Show him the way, Bob," said Lyons.

Goff followed Samuels through the counter flap, past the desks and out through the door at the back of the room. Gordon and Parkinson were close behind.

Beyond the door was a corridor giving access to three empty cells, their iron doors agape. At the far end was a green wooden door which Samuels unlocked and pushed open.

"Lights, Ernie," said Samuels.

Parkinson walked back along the corridor and flicked a switch.

"Mind your head," Samuels said to Goff, stepping through the door and descending a stone spiral stairway. Goff followed him down the steps to a stone archway. To the right of the archway was a doorless white-washed room with a wooden table, three chairs, an aluminium sink and a one-ring gas burner. On the table was a red telephone, an electric kettle, a teapot, two canisters and

106

four mugs on a metal tray. A folded invalid chair leant against the far wall.

Samuels stepped through the archway. Directly ahead was a row of steel bars, stretching from wall to wall and floor to ceiling.

Samuels swung a bunch of keys into his left hand, selected one and unlocked the barred door.

"This is a cage, not a cell," said Goff.

"Used to be a wine cellar," said Samuels. He pulled the door open and tilted his head. Goff stepped inside and the door was locked and tested.

"There's a bell at the back," said Gordon, pointing. "But don't bring us all the way down here just to complain about the cockroaches."

Goff walked to the left-hand back corner of the cell and prodded his foot at a wooden slat covering a hole in the floor.

"En suite," said Gordon.

"Jesus," said Goff.

"Don't think he'll hear you down here," said Parkinson.

The three policemen walked back through the archway.

"What about a cup of tea?" called Goff.

"How many lumps?" shouted one of them. All three laughed.

Goff had taken off his top coat and folded it on the ground in the corner opposite the slatted hole. He sat on the coat, his back to the wall, his feet stretched towards the bars. He had ripped away the bottom of his shirt and was now tearing the cotton into thin strips.

He rose to his feet, shoving the strips into his trousers pocket, when he heard footsteps on the stairs. The same three policemen appeared with Beasley.

"Back to the wall, Tiny," Samuels said to Goff.

Goff retreated from the bars, the door was opened and Beasley entered the cage.

Samuels tested the door and the policemen withdrew.

"What a crib," said Beasley. "Not even a bunk." He walked across to examine the slats. "At least there's a back exit."

"I'm a bit surprised to see you, Graham," said Goff.

"Well, yeah."

"You're supposed to talk some sense into me, are you?"

"Could be, could be." Beasley cupped his ear and made a circling motion around the cage with the index finger of his left hand.

"Sod that," said Goff. He returned to the corner and sat on his coat.

Beasley followed him and stood leaning against the wall.

"They took your coat?" said Goff.

"I never had one."

"You're harder than you look, then. Here." He re-arranged the coat, making room for Beasley to sit.

"Thanks," said Beasley, sitting down. "The Oaf's arrived."

"I can expect a visit then."

"I think they want your name and address first."

"They want to know where to send the remains, do they?"

"Don't say that," said Beasley. "They're just worried, I think. You could be a diplomat or something. He sent someone over to the hospital to go through Toaster's things."

"Who did?"

"That old fella, Horace."

"Any news of Toaster?"

"Nothing they told me."

"And what did you tell them?"

"The truth," said Beasley. "What have I got to hide? That I only met you today, that I used to work with Toaster. We went to school together. What are you doing that for?"

Goff had resumed tearing part of his shirt into strips. He put a finger to his lips. "What did Horace say to you?"

"That I could forget about bail while you were acting the mystery man."

"Well, I'm sorry about that, Graham. The fact of the matter is that I haven't got an address here yet. I'm staying with a friend and I don't want him bothered by this rabble."

"Won't Toaster tell them? I mean, just to get you out?"

"He wouldn't and he can't."

Goff began to insert the strips of cloth between his lips and gums.

Beasley touched him on the arm and mouthed, "What's that for?"

Goff squeezed his upper front teeth between finger and thumb and started to sing:

> We've been together now
> For forty years or more
> And it don't seem
> A day too long.

"Oh," said Beasley. "A sort of gumshield. Will it work?"

"The thought, as they say, is everything."

"Should I do the same?"

"If you sit there nice and quiet, I don't think you'll be bothered."

"Do you think so? I mean, maybe that Horace will stop them. He didn't seem to like Swakely, the sergeant, too much."

"He's an odd one all right. But he wears the blue."

Beasley stood up and walked to the bars. With his back to Goff, he said, "I'm supposed to ring the bell if I can get a name and address out of you. I've got three minutes. It would all go a lot easier for both of us, he said. I mean, I'm just telling you."

"I understand, Graham. And I'm sorry. Did you know Toaster had a bad heart?"

"No, he never mentioned it. Maybe he didn't know himself."

"Maybe it's all bullshit," said Goff.

"Yeah," said Beasley. "Bullshit talks and bullshit walks, across the pages of history."

"My old fella used to say that," said Goff.

Beasley turned from the bars. "Hey," he whispered. "They're coming."

Goff rose to his feet, pushing the pieces of cloth tight against his gums. "Get down there," he said, indicating the spot he had vacated. "If they do go for you, roll yourself into a ball. Protect the head and the goolies. With any luck the rest will mend itself. And Graham –" putting a hand on Beasley's shoulder and giving him a smile distorted by the linen gumshield – "try not to piss on my coat."

Goff moved to the middle of the cage and fastened all four buttons on his jacket. He stretched his arms above his head, wriggled his shoulders, and walked to the bars.

The turnkey, Samuels, was coming through the

110

archway followed by Inspector Grace, Sergeant Swakely and constables Kilbride and Davis. Grace and Swakely carried truncheons covered with black rubber hose.

Samuels produced a plain wooden truncheon as he approached the bars and snapped it at Goff's hands. "Same as last time, Tiny. Right back against the wall. These kind gentlemen want to ask you a few questions."

Goff snatched his hands from the bars and stepped back a pace.

"Beasley," said Samuels. "You're coming out first. Didn't you hear me, Tiny? I said back, right back. Get over there and stand on the bog."

Goff looked at Inspector Grace. "The only shithouse I can see is standing right in front of me," he said.

Grace stepped towards the bars. "Look at the cunt. He can't wait for it."

"What's he been eating?" said Swakely.

"Let me handle this," said Samuels, raising his voice. "I want you right back against the wall," he shouted at Goff. He moved forward to push Inspector Grace away from the bars. "Let's get him back there first and the other one out. There's a right way to do this."

"Kilbride hold your cock while you had a piss, did he?" Goff said to Inspector Grace.

The Inspector grinned at him. "You'll be pissing out of your eyes in a minute."

"He was interested in the colour, weren't you, Will?" Goff said to Kilbride.

"If you don't get back against that wall, I'll take a hand in this myself," Samuels said to Goff.

Goff ignored him. "Usual pale yellow, though, wasn't it, Will?" said Goff. "His piss, I mean. What else could you expect from a scumbag like him?"

Kilbride approached the bars. "You heard him. Get back against that wall."

"For God's sake," said Samuels, tugging at Kilbride's arm. "I explained the procedure."

"Never mind the procedure," said Grace. "You just

get the door open. He's not going anywhere. Except maybe down that hole in the corner."

"Well, get him away first," said Samuels, indicating Kilbride.

Inspector Grace moved up to Kilbride and took his arm. "Just for the moment, Will, we'll play it – hey . . ."

Goff had stepped forward and whipped his right hand through the bars. It locked on the collar of Inspector Grace's jacket. Kilbride lunged between them and Goff's left arm flashed through an adjacent pair of bars, clawing at Kilbride's eyes. Kilbride stumbled backwards, shouting, "Watch him, watch him."

The Inspector tried to pull free. Goff grasped one of the bars with his left fist and used it as a fulcrum. He threw his other hand forward, knocking the Inspector off balance, and then dragged it back towards the bars. The Inspector flung up a hand to protect his face. His head and hand thumped against the bars.

"Fuck, fuck, fuck," screamed Samuels. "I warned you."

The Inspector shouted, "Stop, stop," pushing away from the bars, dropping his truncheon and scratching at Goff's hand and face.

Goff pushed him away again, braced himself, and dragged the Inspector back towards him. The Inspector's left cheekbone cracked against the bar. He flung his fist at Goff and hit him in the mouth.

Goff, his right sleeve spattered with the Inspector's blood, propelled him away from the bars again. The Inspector swayed and began to go limp, pulling Goff's hand downwards. Swakely, pushing Kilbride aside, hacked at Goff's arm with his truncheon. Goff released the Inspector and let his arm swing back inside the bars.

Davis was shouting, "Get it open, get it open," at Samuels, who stared, white-faced, at the crumpled body of Inspector Grace.

Goff began to kick the Inspector through the bars,

hacking down at him with the heel of his shoe. Swakely dragged the Inspector clear and Goff reached through with his left hand and picked up the fallen truncheon. He moved towards the door and stabbed the truncheon through the bars, point foremost, at Davis.

Davis turned his head to one side and the blow caught him in the neck just under the chin. "You cunt," he yelled at Goff, jumping forward, holding the bar with his left hand and swinging at Goff with his right.

Goff, his own right arm slumped against his side, took Davis's blow in the throat. He checked himself and then smashed the truncheon against the knuckles of Davis's left hand, a backhanded blow that left a smear of blood on the bars as Davis snatched his hand away.

Davis, hand to his mouth, was poised to swing again at Goff when Kilbride took him in a bear-hug from behind and hoisted him clear of the stabbing truncheon.

Goff, his face red, veins pulsing in his neck, trilled the truncheon across the bars. "Who's next, then? Who's next?" he shouted, his voice thickened by the blow to the throat. "This is Tom Goff, you scumbags. Tom Goff's the name, blood's the game. Mine or yours. Let's get at it. Who's next, who's next?"

He stood close against the bars, beating them with the truncheon, his teeth grinding, rolling his right shoulder, clenching and unclenching his right fist.

"Fucking hell," said Kilbride, holding Davis. "He's gone bananas."

Swakely, kneeling to cradle the Inspector's head in both hands, shouted at Kilbride, "You were a great help."

Kilbride turned at right angles and pushed Davis towards the stone archway. He turned back and pointed his finger at Swakely. "Don't start on me, Arthur. Just don't start on me. I almost lost my peepers. And who told me and Ron we wouldn't need our truncheons? Who said they'd just be in the way and all we'd have to do was hold him? Who told us that, Arthur? So don't try and blame me for this fucking mess."

Swakely said, "All right, all right. No need to screech. Let's all calm down. Give me a hand here."

Samuels said, "I warned you. I warned you. Don't say I didn't warn you. I kept warning you. Do you think this hasn't happened before? Do you think we don't know what we're doing? But no. You couldn't wait, could you? You just couldn't wait."

"Knock it off, Bob, for fuck's sake," said Swakely. "We can have a post mortem later. Come and give me a hand, Will."

Goff was marching up and down the length of the bars, clouting them with the truncheon. "Tom Goff's the name. Blood's his game. Tom never-had-enough Goff. Tom the terror. Tom thumb-in-your-eye Goff. Look at those pansies, Graham. Look at the heroes, the bully boys, the hard men in blue. Look at them out there bleeding and squealing. Look at their mighty leader. Look at that crap seeping out of his snotbag. Can you imagine what it'll be like when I get them in here? Come in, lads, come in. Look, look, I'll stand over by the wall so you can get safely inside."

He moved to the back of the cell until he was standing on the wooden slats above the hole. "Come on, lads, I'm back here, right out of the way. It's safe. You can come in for nothing. No charge. Come in and say hello to good old Tom. But be kind and polite. Tom Goff can cut up rough."

He went back to the bars and stood opposite Davis. "Hey, Ron."

Davis, fixing a handkerchief around his bleeding knuckles, looked up at Goff. Bits of linen hung from his mouth and two lines of blood ran from his nose. Davis turned away, using his teeth to tie a knot.

"Hey, Ron," said Goff in a music-hall whisper. "Here. Come here." He put his left hand, holding the truncheon, behind his back. "Come on, Ron. It's time for that operation you promised me. Now's your chance, your best bet. I've only got one arm working and I promise not to use the stick. What do you say, Ron? Step this way. Tom Goff's the real stuff."

Swakely left Kilbride with the Inspector and walked across to Davis, positioning himself between Davis and Goff. He examined Davis's hand. "Is it broken?"

"Don't know. Badly smashed anyway. I can't move my fingers."

"We're taking the boss upstairs. Do you think you could manage a leg with your good hand?"

"Why don't we get a stretcher?"

"Because we don't need any fucking help from anybody else, Davis. You got that?"

"Yes, sir, Sergeant Swakely, I've got that. But there's no need to take it out on me, either. Have you got that?"

Swakely patted Davis on the shoulder. "I'm sorry, Ron. We're all a bit ragged. Let's just see what you can manage, okay?"

"A good kick up the arse is what he needs, sergeant," said Goff. "The man's a malingerer. A little slap on the knuckles and what do you get? Gross dereliction of duty. He'll be blubbing in a minute."

Swakely guided Davis towards the group around the Inspector and turned to face Goff. "You're feeling pretty pleased with yourself, aren't you?"

"Can't hear you, sergeant. Come a little closer."

"Pretty damned pleased."

"What's that, sarge?"

Swakely put his hands on his hips and nodded his head towards the Inspector. "But you've really gone and done it now. My, oh my, you've really done it now."

Goff clamped the truncheon across two of the bars and used it as a leaning post, his left hand stretched out, his ankles crossed. "Tell me this, sergeant. How is it that you and Kilbride haven't got a scratch between you? How is that now?"

"He's cute and I'm careful. So, at least we've got a name out of you. Where do you live, Tom Goff?"

"I live in contempt of the likes of you, sergeant. Sergeant Arthur, isn't it? Arfer man and arfer joke."

Swakely smiled and tilted his chin upwards. "That's the way, Tarzan. You enjoy yourself while you've still got a few faculties. Because I promise you this, Thomas old son, you won't be walking out of that cell on your own two legs. This is the last day of your life as a whole man. We'll be back in no time at all, Tom. And this time we'll do it right. I've made two mistakes with you today. I won't make a third. You enjoy yourself now. You've made cunts of us, there's no denying that. But I'm going to make a cripple out of you."

Swakely walked back to the group around the Inspector. "All ready? Nice and easy and together."

They lifted the Inspector and shuffled him through the archway and up the stairs. Goff stood at the bars, the truncheon to his lips, blowing the Entrance of the Gladiators.

He turned and looked at Beasley. "Well, Graham. First round to Goff, wouldn't you say?"

Beasley waved the back of his hand at Goff and turned his head to the wall.

"And what's the matter with you?" shouted Goff.

Beasley swung back towards him, his finger pointing at Goff, his voice high and loud. "You're what's the matter. You. You. You. You crazy sod. I'm locked in a cell with a crazy. That has penetrated your skull, has it? I mean, that we're in a cell. Locked up. Can't go anywhere. Stuck. What in God's name do you think you're doing?"

Goff threw the truncheon at the wall. "You're not hurt, are you?"

"Not hurt? Not hurt? Oh, no, I'm not hurt," said Beasley. He stood up. "I'm not hurt, I'm fucking doomed. They're going to come back, you heard what he said, they're going to come back and they're going to kill us. Not hurt us. Kill us. You're on your own, you are. How could you do a thing like that? You've probably cracked his skull. He might even die. Who's going to worry about us if a Police Inspector dies? What were you doing? What, in God's name, did you think you were doing?"

"Calm yourself."

"What's that?" said Beasley, walking towards him. "What did you say? Calm yourself? You're telling me to calm myself. Tom Goff's telling me to calm myself. Tom the terror. Blood's his game. You're telling me to calm myself?"

Goff put his hands on Beasley's shoulders. Beasley attempted to wrench himself free. Goff held him with his left hand and pulled him closer. "Take it easy now, Graham. Take it easy. This'll do neither of us any good. I admit I got a bit excited back there. It sometimes happens."

"A bit excited? You were bonkers. You should have seen yourself. Your hair standing up, your eyes all over the place, all that cotton froth trailing from your mouth, and your voice . . . You were gone."

Goff turned away, wiping Beasley's spittle from his face. "I was worried about Toaster. You forgotten what that bastard did to Toaster? This is none of our doing. None of it. These people attacked us, insulted us, put Toaster in hospital."

"You were trying to kill him," said Beasley. "Not just hurt him. I mean, you were trying to finish him off."

"I said I got a bit excited. I planned none of it. I just saw the chance there. I just reacted."

Beasley looked out through the bars, his back to Goff. "We're in a cell."

"I know where we are, Graham."

"We can't go anywhere. We can't go for a walk, catch a plane, hide, disappear. We've got to stay here. And they've got to come back. Easy, isn't it? We're prisoners, they're the law. They might be a bunch of scumbags but they can do anything they like to us. They are the law."

"They're just men."

"And you're Tom Goff?"

"That's right."

Beasley dropped his forehead against the bars. "Well, Tom Goff is not John Fucking Wayne and this is not some old fucking Western where all the baddies get shot. You're so fucking strong, aren't you? So tough. Take no shit from anyone. You heard what he said. He'll cripple you. He means it. I know he means it because I know

117

what happened in here. Do you know what happened? You shamed them. They were all ashamed. Do you think that's going to make it any better for us?"

"Is it going to make it any better for Toaster?"

Beasley swung around. "Fuck Toaster. Toaster's not here. We've got to look after ourselves. I mean, they're monsters. Monsters. These people are straight out of nightmares."

Goff took Beasley's head in both hands and wiped his thumbs in an arc across Beasley's cheekbones. "Shape up, now, Graham. They'll be back in a minute. Hold yourself together. We don't want them to think they're winning."

Beasley held Goff's wrists. "Let them think they're winning. Let them win. What's wrong with you? Can't you take a few slaps? Just swallow it. Why didn't you just swallow it? It'd be all over by now. You might be hurting a bit. But so what? What's it matter?"

"Come on, Graham, come on. We're better than that. Where's your pride, your dignity, your sense of right-ness?"

Beasley wrenched Goff's hands away from his neck. "Crap. More fucking crap. How the hell have you lived so long? This is a sewer. We're in a fucking sewer. You get shit in a sewer. Not pride and dignity. Shit. Nothing else."

Goff moved to his left to keep Beasley's face in view. "You mean we're shit? Me and you are shit?"

"Just shit."

"I don't think you're shit, Graham."

"Oh, Christ." Beasley flopped back against the wall and slid down into a sitting position on Goff's coat. "You don't think I'm shit?"

"No."

"There's no end to you, is there? Where do you get off? You don't think I'm shit? You were thinking of me, were you, when you were being upright and heroic? Sense of rightness. That was all for me, was it? Bollocks. I'm the bit part in this act. You can be Horatius all you like, the martyr, the diehard. But don't make out you're doing it all for the sake of the bloody scenery. Spare me the high principles. The only thing that worries me right now, my health – my life, more like it – well, there's no room for that in your epic, is there? You want to be the star in some old-fashioned fantasy? Good. That's good. But I'm locked in here with you and I don't want to know. Nice and slowly now. I'll say this nice and slowly so the message gets across loud and clear. I do not want to be the victim of your fucking conceit. All right? You got that?"

Goff looked out towards the stone archway. "Okay, okay. I should think Quasimodo heard that. There's another piece of shirt in the overcoat pocket there. Why don't you wipe your nose?" He began moving about the cage picking up the strips of linen that had spewed from his mouth. "See, Graham? It's not hard to get excited." He picked up the truncheon.

Beasley fumbled the makeshift handkerchief from Goff's coat and wiped his eyes and nose. Goff stuffed the linen strips into his top pocket and sat down beside him.

"Conceit, eh?" said Goff. "That's a hard one to fight. Like being told you're boring. There's no real come-back. A bit below the belt, that, Graham. You're a vicious man with the verbals."

Beasley blew snot and laughter through his nose and into the handkerchief. "Leave off."

Goff rolled the truncheon to and fro between his legs. "I wasn't thinking of you back then. That's true and I'm sorry about it."

"I'm so fucking scared," said Beasley.

"If Toaster's fit enough to use a telephone we won't be here long."

"Aren't you frightened, Tom?"

"More than a little bit."

"It doesn't show, though. Unless you go berserk to hide it."

Goff flipped the truncheon into a spin. "Take that sergeant. He's got a touch of malice in him. He said he'd cripple me. Now that's something to fear. Being lame. Or impotent. But you can fight that sort of fear by thinking of a worse one."

"Like being dead."

Goff tossed the truncheon into the air, caught it on the end of his finger and held it balanced there. "I don't know about that. They say you can die of fright but I never heard of a corpse being frightened back to life. No. Why don't I take a few slaps, you said. It'd be all over by now. But it wouldn't, see. Not if you kill the temptation with a bigger fear. I thought how bad I'd feel afterwards by lying down to that class of bastard. It'd gnaw away at me for the rest of my life. I terrify myself with a thought like that and taking a few more slaps doesn't seem so bad. Regrets are worse than grazes, as they say."

"Who does?"

"The old fellow again."

"It's not bad, that."

"He was full of them. You can live by the head or by the heart, son, but which gives the worse pain?"

"Same source?"

Goff flipped the truncheon into a somersault and caught it on the back of his hand. "His all-time number one."

"Maybe we should scratch it up on the wall," said Beasley.

"No," said Goff. "I can't spell migraine."

Lyons stepped through the archway carrying three mugs on a tin tray.

Goff, his mouth swollen with cloth, stood at the bars, the truncheon in his left hand.

Beasley sat on Goff's coat in the corner, hugging his knees.

Lyons placed the tray on the ground in front of Goff. He lifted one mug and pushed the tray towards the bars with his feet. He turned, placed his own mug on the flagstones, and walked to the alcove by the archway. He removed the invalid chair, opened it, sat, and wheeled himself back to his mug of tea. "Cheers," he said.

Goff removed the linen strips from his mouth and tucked them into his pocket. "That's supposed to intimidate us, is it?"

"Drink your tea and forget the psychology," said Lyons. He slapped the left arm of the chair. "This is here because you can't get a stretcher up those stairs. You can't expect the cricketers to work that out for themselves – but what was Bob playing at? You must have scrambled his brains."

"Have a bit of trouble, did they?" said Goff.

"Almost scraped his wig off."

"How is he?"

Lyons slurped up tea from his mug. "He'll live. Won't smile for a while."

Goff rolled the truncheon behind him and reached through the bars for the tray. He dragged it towards him, brought the two mugs inside and carried one to Beasley.

"I hear you've been fee-fi-fo-fumming it," said Lyons.
"What's that?"

"Wanting the blood of an Englishman."

"Fee-fi-fo-fum."

"The giant from Jack and the Beanstalk."

"I remember," said Goff. "He died."

"They were the days. Happy endings every time."

Goff sipped his tea and raised the mug. "Stay lucky."

"Thanks, Mr Lyons," said Beasley.

"My pleasure."

"This is all very cosy," said Goff. "Are you the calm before the storm, Horace? The kiss before the blow?"

Lyons scratched his right armpit, spilling tea. "Why didn't you take your lumps and have done with it, Tom?"

"That's what I told him," said Beasley.

"That's right," said Goff, turning to look at Beasley. He faced Lyons again. "So what's your act, Horace? The decent old-fashioned copper with a heart of gold? What do you want?"

"The truncheon. It's government property."

Goff laughed. "Aren't we all? Give me your truncheon and your trust."

Lyons moved the chair forward and sideways with a twist of his left hand. "It won't do you much good. They'll be down with shields and sticks in a minute."

"What are you worried about then?"

"It looks bad on the report, for one thing. But it might cool them down a bit if I take it back upstairs with me."

"They're not going to wait until we fall asleep?"

"They've got no time for that, Tom. This is not their regular nick. They can't hang about. The way things are now, you've got a weapon. A good excuse for them to go over the top."

"And kindly old Horace is only thinking of our welfare."

"You're a contrary bastard," said Lyons. He picked at his nose with his left thumb. "They go too far with you and they're going to leave a mess. Messes have to be cleaned up. I'm planning to take my kids to basketball tonight. I don't want to have to stay on here and clean up a mess."

"He's kind to children, too."

"Give me the truncheon. It might save your life."

Goff picked up the truncheon and twirled it between his fingers. "Save a life? Well, now, that's dramatic enough. I'll tell you what, Horace. Get Graham here into one of those cells upstairs and you can have the stick."

"No one's going to bother him."

"Well, get him out then."

"No, that won't wash."

"It won't, eh?"

"Not if you think about it. They were going to take him out on the last visit and look what happened. It'll be the same again. To get him out we have to unlock the door. To unlock the door we have to be mob-handed down here. Get a mob down here and unlock that door and they'll swarm over you anyway. I'm telling you, though. He'll be all right. Invisible."

"I see."

"Is that a joke?"

"You're a joke, Horace. P C Plod, everyone's friend. Keep the truncheon, nasty mess. Hand it over, nice clean mess. I think I'd rather have them all fired up and pissed off. It won't hurt so much."

"Don't believe it."

"Are you going to be here to keep the chastisement within reasonable bounds?"

Lyons turned the wheel and moved the chair backwards. "That might take some explaining. They'll be making further inquiries. Why should I be here?"

"And why are we here? Down below ground, I mean."

"All the upstairs cells are full. Come on."

"Now it's P C Dodge."

"You're beginning to sound sorry for yourself."

Goff finished his tea and weighed the mug in his hand. "This could make a nasty sort of weapon. Did you consider that, Horace?"

Lyons propelled the chair up to the bars. "I gave it a good five minutes thought. And I came to the conclusion that Tom Goff was a man who wouldn't take advantage of a kindness. A man of honour."

He smiled at Goff and held out his hand.

Goff laughed and handed him the empty mug. "I'll bet you did. You're just a chancer, Horace. You thought you'd buy a truncheon with a cup of tea. What would anybody in a uniform like that – blue for bruises – know about honour?"

Lyons placed both mugs, his own and Goff's, on the ground beside the wheelchair. He took cigarettes and matches from his top pocket, lit one, and dropped the match into one of the mugs. "You take the Oaf, now," he said to Goff. "W.G. Take Arthur, too. And the rest of them. They probably don't seem much to you. A bunch of heavies. Thick and nasty. Which is true enough to a certain extent. But that's the way it is today. It's a nasty, thick old world out there. You'd agree with that, Tom?"

"We're short of handkerchiefs in here, Horace."

Lyons rubbed at the inside of his thigh with his thumb. "I'm just trying to explain something."

"Let's hear him," said Beasley.

"Thank you, Graham," said Lyons. He worked his left hand down under his waistband and adjusted his testicles. "What I mean is, things aren't getting any better. Everybody expects so much these days. That's the real problem. You need the law there to keep the status quo. But your average young copper doesn't think like that. He joins because the money's good, there's some nice perks and the work can be interesting. Maybe you don't want to believe it but a lot of young kids come out of training college bursting, glowing with good intentions. They really want to help make it a good world, a better place for everyone. And what do they find? They find out they're lepers, everybody hates them, they're scum. That's a shock. Some of them leave. The rest of us stay and get introspective. We stick together. We also get a bit sick at the way things are. And when you're sick, you do bad things, silly things. You lose your sense of humour, you lose your patience. Now, with you, Thomas. I don't know what happened in that pub. I don't want to know. You probably got a smack or something and reacted. You provoked somebody. Not deliberately, maybe. But you did something, or said something, that would normally just flow by. But the way things are, because of the frustrations, the contempt we get from everybody, bang, and off it goes. If you'd have had any sense, you'd have swallowed it. But you didn't and you're here and now you've made it worse."

"I'm here because you're sick, Horace. Is that what you're telling me?"

Lyons turned the wheelchair so that he could drop his cigarette stub into one of the empty mugs. "In a way, yes. We're all sick. Everybody's sick. All we've got is each other. I meet a copper, a stranger, I can be sure of one thing. He doesn't think I'm a cunt because I wear this uniform. So, we're loyal to each other. That's our bit of honour if you like. And if you take a crack at a policeman, any policeman – including Arthur and the Oaf and some a lot worse – then I'm on their side. I've got to be. I don't care why you did it or what they did to you. That's the way it is. That's the way it is. It's too late to be fair. It's too one-sided out there."

Goff beat a tattoo on the bars with the truncheon. "Nicely said. Wasn't that wonderfully well delivered, Graham?"

Lyons levered himself onto his feet and sighed. "You want some advice?"

"Hand over the truncheon?"

Lyons smiled. "Sure. Hand over the truncheon. Get an upper-class accent. Stay out of seedy pubs. Turn the other cheek. I don't think you're listening. Let's have that cup, Graham."

Lyons picked up the two mugs by the chair and took the third from Beasley. He held the three mugs in a barman's grip and wheeled the chair back to the alcove. He folded and stacked the chair and waved at them from the bottom step. "Good luck, lads," he said and went up the stairs.

Beasley joined Goff at the bars. "I thought you were going to give him the truncheon."

"No. He's just an actor."

"At least we got a cup of tea."

"He wants something, all right. What did he say to you upstairs? After I'd gone?"

Beasley gripped Goff's upper arm. "Shssh. They're at the top. Talking."

"Must be the rush hour."

"They're coming, they're coming."

"Soft and easy now, Graham. Get back over there and remember what I said about your bladder."

Goff held the truncheon between his legs and stuffed his mouth with the strips of linen.

A laminated glass shield, held by Samuels, came through the archway. Evans followed with another shield. Behind them came Swakely, Kilbride and Swan carrying leather-tipped wooden lances.

Samuels stopped in front of the bars, speaking over the top of his shield. "I'm only going to tell you once," he said to Goff. "Get back over there against the wall."

Goff moved along the bars to get a clearer view of Swakely. "How's good old W.G., sarge? Lost none of his cheek? Putting a brave face on it?"

"Right," said Samuels. He turned to Swakely. "Just remember, keep him away from my pegs."

"And you," said Goff. "Swanny, isn't it? How's your little leggsy weggsy? Bruisy-woosed?"

Evans moved up alongside Samuels, the two shields touching. Swakely and Kilbride took the flanks. Swan waited in the rear.

The two shields crashed against the bars. Swakely and Kilbride thrust their sticks inside the cell at Goff. Samuels, his feet withdrawn, leaning against the shield, guided his bunch of keys towards the lock.

Goff brushed aside the probing sticks and slid in beneath them, slashing through the bars and up under the shield at Samuels.

"Keep him off me," shouted Samuels, pushing his feet further from the bars.

Kilbride's lance hit Goff under the heart. Goff turned, catching the stick between body and arm, trapping it there.

Swan stepped around Evans and stabbed his lance into

the cell, hitting Goff in the throat and knocking him sideways. Goff fell, keeping his lock on Kilbride's stick. Swakely flicked at his groin.

"That's it," shouted Samuels. "Hold him there."

From the floor, Goff raised the truncheon and threw it through the bars. It struck Kilbride just above his nose. He whipped his head back, releasing his lance. Goff was forced against the floor by a poke in the ribs from Swan. Kilbride's stick fell loose across the bottom rung of horizontal bars. Swakely bent to retrieve it and Goff flashed at it with his right foot, hooking it back inside the cell.

The stick landed behind Goff and he turned, reaching towards it. Swakely dropped his own lance and snatched at the bottom of Goff's trousers, holding him pinned against the bars. Goff stretched for Kilbride's lance. It was out of reach. Swan crouched, pushing his arm between the bars, guiding Kilbride's lance further away from Goff. Swakely tightened his grip on Goff's trousers. Goff thrashed and rolled and kicked out with his free leg.

"Graham," said Goff. "Graham."

Beasley, hunched in the corner, elbows on his drawn-up knees, both hands covering his face, looked through his fingers at Goff. The scuffling and the jabbing and the rattling of shields faded into hard, heavy breathing.

Goff's right hand, fingers open, was stretching for the fallen stick. He was bleeding from a cut above the left eye and a small lick of blood was trickling across the eyelid and dripping from the lash.

Beasley's right hand touched the floor and he swayed forward.

"Beasley," screamed Swakely. "Touch that fucking stick and you're a dead man."

Kilbride, a cracked purple star swelling on his forehead, reached past Swakely and gripped Goff's other leg.

"Got him, got him," shouted Kilbride. He squatted down in front of the bars and dragged Goff towards him.

"For fuck's sake, Bob, what are you waiting for?" Swakely said to Samuels.

"Don't sweat, don't sweat," said Samuels. He tossed aside his shield and pulled open the cell door.

Swan rushed into the cell and swept his stick across the back of Goff's head. Goff turned, his arm raised. Swan dropped his lance and aimed a kick at Goff's face. Goff tried to trip him. Swan kicked again.

"Get hold of yourself, Swanny," shouted Swakely. "Leave his boat alone."

Kilbride twisted Goff's leg across the bar and said, "Okay, he's mine now."

"You got him?" said Swakely.

"He's mine, I tell you, he's mine," said Kilbride.

Swakely released his hold on Goff's trousers and ran into the cell. Samuels followed. Swakely kicked Goff in the ribs and dropped to his knees, holding Goff by the throat and punching at his body. Samuels stepped past Swakely and pinned Goff's legs to the floor. Kilbride, smiling, unsheathed his truncheon and walked into the cell.

"Give me room, Arthur," said Kilbride. He began hacking at Goff's thighs and groin with his truncheon.

Goff had ceased to struggle. Blood, vomit, grunts and whimpers came from his mouth.

"Don't forget the kidneys, Will," said Swakely.

"Too many fucking cooks," said Kilbride.

Samuels stood up and left the cell. Kilbride changed his stance, sweeping the truncheon down across his body into Goff's kidneys.

"Now who's changing colour?" said Swan.

"You'll kill him," said Evans. He was still outside the cell, holding his shield.

Swakely looked at him. "We'll just about."

"It's never worth it," said Evans. "He's had enough."

"Hold up, Will, maybe he's right," said Swakely. "But give me that a minute. I've got a promise to keep. Stretch his arms back at the top."

Kilbride sat behind Goff's head, his feet on Goff's shoulders, pulling on both his arms.

"Roll up his trousers," Swakely said to Swan. "Above the knee."

Swan knelt to push Goff's trousers up around his calfs.

"That'll do," said Swakely. He turned Goff's leg off its heel and tilted the body sideways so that the knee was lying flush to the floor. He crashed his truncheon down on the inside of the knee. Goff's mouth trembled and opened.

"He whinnied," said Swan. "Like a fucking horse. Did you hear that bone crack?"

Swakely walked around behind Kilbride, adjusted Goff's other leg and smashed its kneecap. "I said I'd cripple the bastard." A drop of sweat fell from his nose and broke on the truncheon in a tiny rainbow.

Kilbride dropped Goff's arms and squatted over his chest. He pinched Goff's top lip between his fingers and squeezed. "He's well gone. I thought he'd last longer."

"And I thought I'd get more satisfaction," said Swakely. He handed Kilbride the truncheon and rolled Goff's trousers down to his boots.

"We could do the soles of his feet to be sure," said Swan.

"I'm sure," said Swakely. "Cuff him, though. We don't want more nonsense if the guv'nor feels up to a visit."

"Cuff him?" said Samuels. "Leave it out, sergeant. He'll be as tame as a lamb for months."

Swakely said to Kilbride, "Cuff him, Will," and stepped outside the cell, his face close to Samuels. "He took a good few digs in the pub and was as frisky as a fucking horse within half an hour."

Kilbride rolled Goff onto his stomach and dragged his arms together. "We should have plastic-bagged the bastard a few times." He fitted handcuffs on Goff's wrists and clicked them closed.

Samuels stepped into the cell. "Just a minute, Will."

Kilbride tested the handcuffs, chafing them against Goff's skin.

"I said just a minute," said Samuels. "You. Kilbride."

Kilbride swung around at him. "What's your problem?"

Samuels spoke to Swakely through the open cell door. "I'm not having him cuffed."

"You what?"

Samuels rolled Goff onto his side and lifted his right eyelid. "I don't like the look of him for one thing. And Horace won't wear it for another."

"Well, I'll be fucked," said Swakely.

"So you may be if he dies," said Samuels. "But, what's more important, Sergeant, so shall I."

"This is a big strong boy," said Kilbride. "You saw what he got up to."

"He's not being cuffed and that's the end of it."

"Because Horace won't like it," said Swakely.

"I said that's one of the reasons."

"Horace run this nick, does he?"

"He gets listened to."

"What's he got?" said Kilbride. "A bleeding megaphone?"

"He can whisper louder than you can shout, Kilbride," said Evans.

"Oh, yeah?" Kilbride approached the bars. "And how would you know, Taffy?"

"I've worked with him."

"Have you? Well, you're working with us now. And you'd better know about my whisper. It leaves a ringing in your ears."

"Knock it off, Will," said Swakely.

"I'll knock something off," said Kilbride.

Samuels said, "What he means is that you can hear Horace's whisper coming out of the mouth of the commander."

"We'd better get them off, then, hadn't we?" said Swakely. "Don't want to be upsetting Horace."

"What sodding commander?" said Kilbride. "That cunt Walker?"

"Just take them off, Will," said Swakely.

"Stroll on," said Kilbride. He pushed past Samuels and bent over Goff to remove the handcuffs.

Samuels stood with hands on hips watching Kilbride. He swung around to Beasley. "On your feet, Jack Horner. You get the honeymoon suite upstairs."

Beasley stood and walked to the cell door.

"Is this your coat?" said Samuels.

Beasley shook his head, swallowed and pointed at Goff.

"Wait up then," said Samuels. He picked up the coat, shook it and spread it open on the ground. He moved to Goff, turned him on his back and slid his hands beneath Goff's shoulders. "Let's lay him on the coat," he said to Kilbride.

"Go fuck yourself."

Samuels sighed and looked through the bars at Evans. "Ernie."

Evans balanced his shield against the bars and entered the cell.

"You, too, Gordon – sorry, Graham. Give us a hand," said Samuels.

They lifted Goff and carried him to his coat. "Give his mouth a wipe," Samuels said to Beasley.

"Come on, come on," said Swakely.

Samuels looked around the cell and picked up the truncheon Goff had thrown at Kilbride. He tapped it against his left hand and examined the tip. "Better than a boomerang this, Will. Bounced right off your head and back inside. Not damaged, though. Your guv'nor's, ain't it?"

Kilbride turned away from him.

Samuels stabbed at Kilbride with the truncheon, hitting him twice on the shoulder. "I said ain't this your guv'nor's lost tool?"

Swakely stepped between them and took the truncheon from Samuels. "I'll look after that, Bob. Let's all cool down, eh?" He threw the truncheon through the cell door.

Samuels shrugged and smiled at Kilbride. He took Beasley's arm and steered him out of the cell. "You take him on up, Ernie," he said to Evans. "I've got to lock the door."

Swakely, Kilbride and Swan collected the shields and sticks as Evans led Beasley up the stone stairs. Samuels locked and tested the door.

"Don't forget that truncheon," he said to Kilbride.

Kilbride looked at him through the glass shield. "I don't forget much, Bob."

"Hey, Tom," said Toaster, squeezing the inside of Goff's thigh. "You're not going akip, are you?"

Goff snapped his knuckles at Toaster's hand. "You'll regret that later, Kendellan."

"I'm regretting it already," said Toaster, sucking the back of his glove. "You said let them settle in. They ought to be raising a family by now. Do you want to see this car or not?"

"Indeed I do. But don't you be forgetting I've got delicate joints."

"Let's give them a stretch."

Goff slid open the van door and climbed down onto the car park. Toaster followed. Goff held the door and said to Beasley, "Four quick beeps if there's any movement, Graham."

"Four. Right."

Beasley locked the door behind them and watched through the wing mirror as Goff and Toaster rounded the back of the van. He bent his head towards the radio, edging into another channel. He adjusted the volume and sat back, shoulders against the door, left leg along the seat. He took matches and cigarettes from the top pocket of his dungarees, lighting the cigarette and placing the spent match back inside the box. He left the box open on his lap, flicking the ash on top of the matches as he smoked.

Toaster led Goff to the alleyway at the back of the car park. Goff tapped him on the shoulder and touched a finger to his mouth. He moved off along the warehouse wall, signalling Toaster to stay.

Goff returned within a minute. "I was just checking on that dosser."

"He's gone, has he?"

"He's gone."

They walked through the alleyway and came into a narrow side street, flanked by the car park and warehouse on one side and a line of boarded-up shops on the other. Toaster pointed to a line of four cars parked to their left. "Ours is the Granada."

Goff walked to the car and put his hand under the rear nearside mudguard. He sawed his hand backwards and forwards and brought out a key.

"You know me too well," said Toaster.

"That's where bank clerks hide their keys," said Goff. He unlocked the car, started the engine and revved it up. He studied the controls and flicked two switches. The windscreen-wipers came on. Goff got out of the seat and walked around the car, checking the lights. He returned to the driver's seat. "The petrol gauge?"

"I filled it myself, Tom."

"It's good. I like it," said Goff. He turned off all the controls and locked the door. He attached the key's magnetic hold to the underseal between the front and back door. Still crouched, he glanced up at Toaster and said, "You looked at the boot?"

"Come off it, Tom. No body, no boodle," said Toaster. "That leg-blasting crap. I've been thinking about that. You're trying to jar up Graham, are you?"

Goff's eyes searched the street and he started back towards the alley. "I want to be sure he'll hold together."

"Don't fret. He'll surprise you."

"I don't mean tonight, Toaster. When they talk to him later."

"He's like a conker. Stick him in the oven and he just gets harder and harder. Impossible to crack."

"I preferred vinegar myself."

Toaster laughed. "That goes without saying, Tom. But this is no time to be having second thoughts. You had all your faculties when you agreed to take him."

Goff paused as they turned into the alleyway. "You pressured me. You said he needed to come."

"What?" said Toaster. "I pressured you? Whoever pressured Tom Goff?"

Goff walked ahead. "We all go soft some time or other, Toaster. It's like the poet said, a vague feeling of regret for something you can't quite remember."

"Jesus," said Toaster. "A popular theme that. Shall we stop and look at the stars?"

Goff stopped and looked up at the sky as they entered the car park. "It's a fine night, right enough," he said, grinning.

"What happened in that cellar, Tom?"

"They broke my knees and cracked his ego," said Goff. He turned towards the club and dragged Toaster into a crouch. "Get down. There's someone coming out."

In the van, Beasley crushed the cigarette stub into the matchbox and wound up the window. A slab of light crept across the warehouse wall. A door banged and someone shouted, "Come on, Phil." Three men came out of the club, one of them walking backwards. A fourth man appeared, trotting.

Beasley peered through the windscreen, his hand hovering over the horn. He looked at both wing mirrors.

The four men had gathered around the Land Rover. Two of them lit cigarettes. Someone said, "You've got to promise no detours. Promise me that, Harry, no detours." A mumble and a splutter of laughter and they began to enter the vehicle, three in the front, one in the rear. The engine started and the lights came on. The driver played with the engine. Funnels of white plumed from the exhaust pipe. A lighted cigarette arced back towards the club. The Land Rover jumped forward, slowed and curved towards the van.

Beasley ducked his head as the vehicle swept past and out of the car park.

Goff tapped on the passenger door window with his nail. Beasley jerked his head at the noise and slid across the seat to lift the catch. Goff climbed into the cab and

134

pointed at the other door. Beasley unlocked it. Toaster entered, sitting behind the wheel, leaving Beasley in the middle.

"Why didn't you beep?" said Goff.

"It wasn't them."

"You couldn't know that."

"One of them was looking this way. It might have been suspicious."

Goff grunted and brushed at the windscreen with the back of his glove. "I hope you were careful with that cigarette."

"I was. Don't worry."

Toaster pushed his face close to Beasley's and narrowed his eyes. "It's the quiet that worries me."

Beasley smiled and shook his head. "Come the dawn, son, and you'll be praying for a moment like this."

Goff turned to look at them. "What's with you two?"

Toaster laughed. "Just our little tribute to the motion-picture industry, Tom."

"What?"

Toaster spread his hands. "It's the lull before the action. A bit of dialogue to give somebody a chance to moralize. Helps build up the tension. The rat asks and the bear answers."

"Sweet Mother of God."

"Don't get pissed off, Tom. It's only a game. I'm the rat, see. Sly, wicked, untrustworthy. And you're the bear. Big, honest and brave. And I'm cracking up and say, 'Why us? Why does it have to be us?' and you say, well, what do you say, Tom?"

"You're a grave disappointment to me, Toaster."

"Well?" Toaster said to Beasley. "Pretty pathetic. Five?"

"No, six," said Beasley. "At least one for sincerity."

"And another for the mad gleam in the eyes," said Toaster.

"Look," said Goff. "If you two are feeling nervous, take a walk. I don't want you getting hysterical in here."

"It's just a bit of fun, Tom," said Toaster.

"All right."

Beasley coughed. "Four of them took off in the Land Rover. I think the extra man was Davis. I'm pretty sure it was Davis."

"Not Kilbride or Swakely?" said Goff.

"Definitely not."

"So, we're down to three," said Toaster.

"That makes you feel better, Graham?" said Goff.

Beasley strummed the air with his right hand and sang, "Three was never enough for the boys who followed Goff."

Toaster groaned. "That's a minus, Beasley."

Goff closed his eyes.

"Only trying to smile in the face of death, Mr Goff," said Beasley.

"Dreamers smile, heroes squawk," said Goff.

"What's that?"

"One of the old fellow's?" said Beasley.

"No," said Goff. "It's from a combat manual. Korean. 'When taken by stealth and death is inevitable, a good soldier will attempt some noise, even a squawk, to alert his comrades.' The louder you die, the braver you are."

"Not bad, not bad," said Beasley. "Even a squawk."

"An easy nine, Tom," said Toaster. "When were you learning stuff like that?"

"Long ago, Toaster. Before I grew up. What's the time?"

Toaster glanced at the dashboard. "Ten past one."

"You happy with the second car?" Beasley said to Goff.

"Yes," said Goff. "I like it. Fast and discreet. In fact, I think we should take it no matter what."

"You mean leave the van even if there's no trouble?"

"That's right. They're both from the airport, Toaster?"

Toaster was adjusting the radio dial. "Long-term. I saw both owners check in. They should be good for a few days. Me and Stokesy had them both away this morning. Or rather, yesterday morning. I wish you'd leave the radio alone, Graham."

136

"That's what we'll do then," said Goff, tightening his gloves on the inside of his fist. "You paying attention, Toaster? No prints, no sweet-papers, you haven't gobbed anywhere?"

"Not me," said Toaster.

"What about you, Graham? You've got that fag-end?"

"In the matchbox. And the ash."

"That's good."

Toaster swung around and peered over the back of the seat. "They should be out within the hour. Don't you think you ought to prepare the Remington, Tom?"

Goff reached behind the seat and dragged the plastic bag to the passenger's side of the van. "You're gun-happy, Toaster. She's primed already."

"Oh? Nothing to fit?"

Goff kissed his teeth. "The stock folds over the receiver and along the barrel. You don't think I'd carry a seven-year-sentence around the streets without some sort of edge, do you?"

"I must confess, I did think it was odd, Tom. Bad camouflage, says I to myself. Why not a flower box or a cricket bag?"

"Poor access."

"I thought maybe you had a little pistol secreted somewhere, Tom."

"Toaster, sometimes I think you belong in a comic book. Why don't you try and rest the lids, like Graham. Leave the watching and the worrying to me."

Toaster looked at Beasley and jabbed him with his elbow. "You're not really having a snooze, are you?"

"It's the music. I'm expiring."

"The music's okay."

"Sure. I always kip before a crisis," said Beasley.

Beasley

Beasley lay on his back with his hands behind his head. He watched the spyhole wink shut and waited on the bunk until the key was in the lock. He was standing when Samuels opened the cell door.

"All change," said Samuels.

Beasley rubbed his face, trailing fingers down the corners of his eyes. "What time is it?"

"Time you answered a few questions. Come on."

Beasley walked past him into the corridor. "How's Goff?"

"Tom the terror? Don't worry about him. He'll live."

Samuels escorted Beasley into the charge room through the rear door. Lyons and Overland were at the counter. Lyons, jacket open, was scratching his buttocks. He turned as the door opened, jerking his head to the right. "Number one, please, Bob."

"This way," said Samuels. He squeezed Beasley's arm and steered him towards a brown door. A white, painted sign said *Interview Room One*. Samuels opened the door and pushed Beasley forward. "Take a pew. He won't be a moment." He left, locking the door behind him.

The only furniture in the room was a wooden table and three chairs. An empty cigarette packet lay in an ashtray on the table. The floor was littered with stubs. Opposite the table, an old-fashioned snake radiator was coiled below the grilled window. Two posters, one on crime prevention, the other on the Colorado beetle, were taped to the lime-green wall behind the table.

Beasley climbed onto the radiator to reach the window. It was raining outside and the drops were forming rivulets against the glass.

"I don't know what's more depressing," said Lyons, behind him. "The view itself or the fact that you can't see it." He was standing in the doorway, a key in his left hand and two mugs of tea in the other. He worked the door shut with his foot and put the key in his pocket. He placed both mugs on the table and sat in the chair nearest the wall.

Beasley jumped off the radiator.

"If you drag the table over there, put a chair on the table, stand on the chair and then – if you're six foot three or taller – you can just catch a glimpse of some scaffolding," said Lyons. "Come and have a cup of tea, son."

Beasley sat facing Lyons and sipped the tea. "No chance of something to eat, is there?"

"No chance is spot on. We're too small for a canteen. We bring our own sarnies and mine are long gone. But you behave yourself and you'll be out of here in no time. Tea all right, is it?"

"Sure."

"That's good," said Lyons. "That's good. Let's get the crap out of the way first."

Lyons took a white envelope from his jacket pocket and shook it. A plastic sachet containing a latchkey fell onto the table. "Seen that before?"

Beasley shook his head. "Not mine."

"I didn't say it was yours. I said have you seen it before. Take a close look."

Beasley half-rose from his chair and leaned across the table. "No. A key's a key. It means nothing to me."

"Pick it up, Graham. Examine it."

Beasley picked up the plastic sachet and held it between his eyes and the fluorescent light. "No. Sorry."

"All right. Put it back."

Beasley replaced the key on the table. Lyons edged the bag back inside the envelope with the top of his pen. "Didn't know you were left-handed, Graham."

"Still a crime, is it?"

"Never was in my book."

Lyons walked to the door and opened it. Samuels was standing outside. Lyons handed him the envelope and closed the door. He sat down and took out a notebook. "Right. Let's try and get through this without the bull-shit."

"That suits me."

"We'll see. You said you didn't know Goff until today?"

"Correct."

"Toaster introduced you. In the pub?"

"I told you."

"And you used to work with Toaster in the res-taurant?"

"That's right."

"What's his proper name?"

"Toaster?"

Lyons looked up from the book and began to clean his ear with the bottom of his pen. "You've been sitting on a four-leaf clover all day, Graham. Blood and breakages all around and you haven't had a scratch. By rights you should have had a hiding just for associating with naughty men. But everybody's been very kind. Now I ask you a simple question and you go all coy. It says here, Graham, it says here where I've written down what you told me earlier, it says here that you went to school with Toaster. But you're having trouble remembering his name."

"He was a form or two behind me at school. Who takes notice of kids in the lower classes? His name was Conningham or Collingdale, something like that. It wasn't till he came to the restaurant that I knew him better. And then he already had the name Toaster. You know what a toaster is? He plays the records, you know, like a D.J. Except he does a bit of his own thing over the top. Talks or sings while the record's playing. All the black clubs have them."

"Oh, got his name in a black club, did he? Which one?"

"It doesn't have to be a club. A blues party, you know."

"No, I don't know."

"Course you do. A drinks party. You pay for the drinks inside. It's a private house. Who are you kidding?"

Lyons pushed his thumb around the inside of his right nostril.

"That's straight," said Beasley.

"And what's Toaster's relationship to Goff?"

"I'm not sure. Second cousin, something like that."

"They're actually related?"

"I thought you knew."

"More important, how do you know?"

"Toaster told me. When Goff was getting the drinks. I think he said their mothers were cousins."

"What else were you talking about?"

"In the pub?"

Lyons flicked his thumb against his index finger and wiped his hand on the side of his trousers. "I have warned you not to fuck about, Graham."

"Well, it was just idle chat. We talked a bit about joggers."

"Joggers?"

"You know, those fat little bald people who run around the parks."

"What about them?"

"Just how horrible they are. Mr Goff had been abroad, you know, and he noticed them more since he got back."

"How long had he been abroad?"

"Four years I think Toaster said."

"You didn't ask Goff himself?"

"No. You don't. He's not the sort, is he? I mean, asking personal questions."

"Where had he been?"

"I don't know that either. He never mentioned it himself. He's been back about a month, though. At least, that's what Toaster said."

"What else did Toaster say?"

"Nothing. He clammed up when Mr Goff came back to the table. He wasn't taking liberties either."

"And what about Goff? Didn't he say anything?"

"He just asked about the restaurant, that's all."

"Come on."

"Look, he was just a stranger in the pub. We had a mutual acquaintance, that's all."

"Think, Graham, think hard."

"Well, he believes in the dignity of man."

"What?"

"Just a joke."

Lyons stood up and walked around the table to stand behind Beasley's chair. He tapped Beasley on the head with his pen. "You're the only joke in here, Graham." He stopped and stepped away. "My God, son, you whiff a bit strong. A bad joke, that's what you are, Graham, a stinker."

Beasley swayed forward on his chair and looked over his shoulder at Lyons. "It was something he said in the cell. When I told him to stop behaving like a hero. He asked me where my dignity was. Said there was some things you didn't lie down for."

"Much good it did him."

"That's what I said."

Lyons walked across to the window and sat on the radiator. He rested his left ankle on his knee, scratching the inside of his sock, stretching his fingers down underneath his instep. "Impressed you, did he?" He spoke with the pen in his mouth.

Beasley turned in his chair, resting his face on its back. "Well, he does have a sort of style. He made me frightened for myself."

"That's right. A man like that could be the death of you, Graham. Still could."

"What do you mean?"

Lyons pushed himself away from the radiator, stamping his left foot on the floor. "Don't get anxious, son, don't get anxious. I'm still trying to get hold of something. Because he impressed me, you see. Tom Goff. Oh, yes. Very much. An easy head, I thought at first. A sweet head. A honeysuckle head. And something more, something sinister, maybe. No identification, no labels. He

145

made the hairs on the back of my neck break into a barn
dance. And that's something I never ignore. No, there's a
suggestion of the very dodgy about Tom Goff. Maybe
something very big, too. But you can't help, can you?
You hardly know him, Graham. Is that right?"

"I keep telling you."

Lyons returned to the table, tapping the pen against his
chin. He sat down. "That's a pity. You see, I was hoping
you'd give me something substantial. An address. Another
name. Something to get to grips with. Something that
could have sent you sailing out of here with all charges
dropped and forgotten. You know what I mean,
Graham?"

"I think so."

"I'm not interested in you, son. A poxy waiter who
can't smell his own piss. You're one of life's losers,
Graham, and I'm a soft-hearted man."

"If I could help, I would."

"Where does Toaster live?"

"Well, he used to live in Milford Lane. Number eighteen. But I think he's moved. He's got a little video business now. I'm not sure where, though."

"You're not sure, you don't know, you'd help if you
could."

Beasley shuffled his chair closer to the table. "Now
just a minute. I go into a pub this afternoon – pub I've
never used before in my life. I go in there because the
marchers are getting out of order and I don't want to be
mistaken for an ordinary, decent citizen and get my head
caved in. I go into the pub and I see Toaster who I went
to school with, who used to work in our restaurant, who
I haven't seen for two years, who buys me a drink and
says come and meet my uncle. And we're all drinking
together for ten or fifteen minutes and suddenly in comes
the law whacking anything that moves. Give me the
marchers anytime. The next thing I know is that I'm
nicked and now I'm here. And that's it. I mean, that's the
truth, there just isn't anything more. Do you want me to
make things up?"

146

"What were you doing there?"

"There's a comic shop about four doors away from the Castle. I was in there. I use it all the time. I'm a collector. Take me home and I'll show you my collection."

"What did you buy?"

"Nothing. They had nothing new."

"And you never use that pub. It being so handy and all. That's odd."

"Look, officer, I never use pubs. If I want a drink I can take my pick of the world's finest wines. Come on."

Lyons dropped his pen on the notebook, tilted his chair back towards the wall and ruffled both hands through his hair. "So, where are we? Toaster's not a close friend of yours. Before today you hadn't seen him for two years. You're not sure of his last name, you've never known his first."

"Yes, yes, yes."

Lyons dropped his chair back on its legs and stood up. He walked halfway around the table, leaning on the edge with one hand, the other on the back of Beasley's chair. "In that case I don't feel so bad having to tell you that Toaster's D.J. days are over. Unless he's into harp music. Get my drift, Graham?"

"He's dead?"

"That was quick. Which Toaster can never be again. Yes, it's sad. Poor old sod's brown bread. Toaster is toasted. Need a while to mourn alone, Graham?"

"He was a good bloke."

"But you hardly knew him."

"You cunt."

Lyons caught Beasley by the hair and wrenched his head across the back of the chair. "What's that, you little shit? What did you say?"

Beasley flailed both hands behind his neck, tugging at Lyons' wrist. "Just because I didn't see him every weekend doesn't mean he wasn't a good bloke. Don't you know anything?"

"No need to shout, Graham." Lyons released Beasley's

hair, wiping his hand on Beasley's shoulder. "Death is man's best friend."

"Sure."

Lyons walked back to his chair and sat down. "It's true that. We'd be knee-deep in geriatrics for one thing. And what would we do for a great sacrifice?"

"Sure."

"No feeling for religion, eh?"

Beasley groomed his hair into place with his hands. "Goff said you were an actor."

"Did he? At the moment I'm being my natural nasty self. Give me a chance to warm up."

"You were just putting it on."

"Downstairs, you mean? One of my favourites, that. Didn't work with that hardhead, though, did it? He wouldn't give a dose to a whore."

"What a bullshitter."

Lyons held the back of his collar away from his neck with his left hand and scraped the pen between his shoulder blades with his right. "Bullshit? That's pretty serious that. But I don't expect to be censured for bull-shitting an enemy of the state."

"Enemy of the state. That's a good one."

Lyons straightened his body and examined the tip of his pen. He began scraping it along the inside of his fingernails. "You need educating, Graham. You want to learn from what you hear. Had a bit of style, did he? Kept going right to the end? Believed in man's dignity? You've missed the real point there, son. That man Goff suffers from a dangerous disease. You know what it is? He believes in justice, Graham. It's worse than rabies."

"He never mentioned justice to me. But so what, anyway? You mean he's like those young coppers you were telling us about? Coming out of training college and wanting to improve the world."

Lyons laughed. "They're kids, Graham. They're entitled to their delusions. You're no kid. And you've got at least ten years on Goff. The pair of you ought to know better."

148

"I can't believe this."

Lyons looked down at his hand. "Christ, look what I've done." He held his hand up to Beasley, the nails new-mooned in ink. "Biro-blue. Still, maybe the wife'll like it."

"Am I going to be charged or not," said Beasley.

Lyons threw the pen onto the table and stood up. "Charged? Did you say charged, Graham? By God, you're being charged all right. Every smartarse comment you make goes into the big book. We're just waiting the moment, me and you. We're just biding our time."

"With a little discussion about justice."

Lyons sucked at his fingers and rubbed them against his jacket. "Why not? It's one of my best themes." He walked around the table to the window and sat on the radiator. "You should see the way they all scarper when I get started down at the club. But you can't do that, Graham, you're –"

"I know. I'm a captive audience."

Lyons rode his buttocks along the radiator ridges. "Don't nick my lines, kid. That's another mark in the book. Your job is to listen and give the odd wise nod of agreement. All right? Yes, justice. Ties in very nicely with what I was saying about the status quo. If everybody starts demanding justice, where are we going to be? They'll be saying he's got a job, I want a job; he's got a house, I want a house; he's got his kids at a good school, I want my kids at a good school; he's got a car, a telephone, hot water, an inside loo, a class accent, a pretty wife, prospects, friends. Where's it all going to end, Graham? No, no. I'll tell you where. In revolution, that's where. The fucking left-wingers will take over. We'll all be out at Highgate every weekend cleaning up the Karl Marx grave. Justice, Graham, is inimical – not bad that, without a stripe to my sleeve – inimical to our way of life. I mean, fair's fair – but nothing fucking else is."

"Brilliant," said Beasley.

"Hold up, hold up. I haven't finished. Half the joy of having a few bob tucked away, a flash motor, the kids at

Eton, a cottage in the country – half the fucking joy is knowing that nearly everybody else can't afford it and will never have it. So when a big-muscled loudmouth like your mate Goff goes around preaching justice, he's attacking the system, the status quo. He's an enemy of the state, Graham, and I'm not joking."

"But he never mentioned justice."

"No, maybe he didn't. But he expects it, Graham. He expects it. And he kicks up when he don't get it. And that's worse. A huge sod like that can make a lot of waves."

Beasley laughed. "You're crazy. What about the politicians? Who's going to beat the shit out of them?"

Lyons pushed himself away from the radiator, his arms crossed on his chest, thumbs flexing into his armpits. "You understand fuck all. The politicians are in the system. The system corrupts if it's given a chance. And it usually is. Look at all your Labour millionaires. I was once pure of heart, Graham. Do you remember that song, 'Around the world, I searched for you,' remember that? I used to believe things like that. You know what I mean. That's how I keep a peg on corruption. I think how I used to be. Like your mate Goff, maybe. He's not in the system. He's a fucking outlaw. I can smell it. He's a dangerous outlaw."

"That's stupid."

Lyons walked back to his chair and sat down. "That won't get me annoyed. You want to do this job for a while, son. You'd experience a whole new dimension to the word stupidity. And thank God for it. Ignorance and apathy. Thank God for them, too. There's little enough to go around without the mob demanding a fair share."

"I always wondered what I lacked," said Beasley.

Lyons put his left hand inside the waistband of his trousers and scratched at his groin. "You lack a lot of things, Graham. A sense of survival for one."

"Meaning?"

"I'm going to get Goff locked up for a long time. And it would be no trouble at all to send you down with him."

"Oh? What have I done?"

"Anything that comes into my head. You understand that?"

Beasley looked up at the ceiling. "There's no justice."

Lyons laughed. "Not bad, Graham, not bad at all." He looked at his watch. "I'm trying to cut down on the fags. It's killing me either way." He took cigarettes and matches from his jacket pocket and lit one, tossing the spent match towards the radiator.

"And what are you doing Goff for?" said Beasley.

"Manslaughter."

"Jesus. Is the Oaf dead, too."

"The Oaf? He'll be as good as new after a visit to Madame Tussaud's. No, Graham, I mean Toaster."

"Toaster?"

"That's right. You remember Toaster? Your mate? He got into a fight with Goff in the pub, didn't he? Lost his ear-ring – sounds odd that – plenty of blood loss, shock, etcetera. Dodgy heart and now the poor boy's dead. I told you that, Graham."

"You said he was dead."

"And his tragic end shall not go unpunished."

"I don't get it."

"All right. Nobody's claiming that Goff meant to kill him, that he knew about the lump in his pump. But it's still manslaughter, unlawful death. He'll cop a handful."

"Someone's been having you on."

"What? Having me on? You mean the boy's not dead at all?"

"Cut it out. I mean, they've been telling you a fantastic story. Goff and Toaster? No way. It's ridiculous. It just won't wash. It was the Inspector. Goff never touched Toaster."

Lyons picked up his pen, retracted the point and began probing into his ear. "Aah, yes. When I first heard the tale I did have my suspicions. After all, they're a mean bunch, the cricketers. Bad aura about them. No great credit to the force. Maybe there's more to this than meets the eye, I told myself. Perhaps I should check up on this.

151

So I did. And I was relieved that the barman was on hand to corroborate the police statements. But even then I felt a slight unease. After all, perhaps the barman had been intimidated."

"If he said that, he's been brainwashed," said Beasley.

"Yes, that too. Or maybe he was just an old crony of the cricketers, only too pleased to perjure himself on their behalf. Dig deeper, Lyons, I told myself. Unearth the truth. And it wasn't until I read the statement of their friend, the man who had been sitting there with the two of them, sharing a drink and trying to smooth over their quarrel, no, it wasn't until I read that statement that I was finally convinced that Goff and Toaster really had come to blows. And with such an unfortunate outcome."

"Oh yeah? What friend is this?"

"There was somebody else there with them, a friend to both, with no axe to grind, a man whose evidence will be accepted by one and all as utterly impartial."

"Oh no there won't."

"What's that?"

"You've got the wrong boy. Shove it."

"I'm only thinking of you, Graham."

"Bollocks."

"Now don't make me angry, son."

"I'm not wearing it."

"I thought you only met him today?"

"That's right."

"Well, he's nothing to you, then, is he?"

"What sort of shit do you think I am? Your fucking Inspector killed Toaster."

"That's a very serious allegation, Graham. Very serious. That sort of outburst can only get you into trouble. More trouble."

"Big deal. Drunk and disorderly. I can handle that."

"There's other charges."

"What charges? Assaulting a police officer, I suppose. I can swallow that, too. I might even have something to say about what's going on in here if you try fitting me up."

Lyons stood up. He examined the tip of his pen. "Tut, tut, tut. I thought you'd be reasonable, Graham. No, wait, I tell a lie. I hoped you'd be reasonable. Naturally, I kept other options open."

"What other options?"

"I'll show you, shall I?" Lyons walked to the door, opened it and shouted, "Bob."

Lyons left the door ajar and turned back to Beasley. "If the worst comes to the worst," said Lyons, "we'll have to settle for a couple of GBHs against Goff. He might get away with eighteen months. He'll probably be out long before you, Graham."

"Oh, yeah? What am I going to get eighteen months for? Refusing to make a false statement?"

Lyons stood at the door with both thumbs in his nostrils. He used his index fingers to move his nose backwards and forwards. He removed his thumbs, sniffed, and wiped them against his trousers. "More wit," he said.

He moved back to the table and picked up his notebook. "Where is it? Here we are. Yes, just over a year ago. You were convicted of possessing a dangerous drug, namely cannabis. Nine months suspended for two years. The two years isn't up, Graham. So that'll be nine months to start with."

"I get it."

"Good."

Samuels knocked on the open door. "Horace."

"Where is he?" said Lyons.

"He's all ready," said Samuels. "Thought I'd better tell you, though. Osborne, the flash brief, he's back and giving Peter a roasting. Maybe you'd better have a word."

"Osborne?"

"Yeah."

"Damn it. All right, Bob, I'll come now." Lyons picked up the notebook and took a key from his pocket. "Won't be a tick," he said to Beasley, locking the door behind him.

Beasley lit one of Lyons' cigarettes and read about the potato pest. He climbed onto the table and looked through the window. It was still raining outside. He could see a warehouse and the skeleton of a tree. He stubbed the cigarette against the wall and dropped the butt.

He jumped from the table and sat on the chair, pocketing the cigarettes and matches. He turned towards the door as the key scraped into the lock.

Lyons was followed into the room by a bearded man in a green three-piece tweed suit. Lyons sat behind the desk and waved his hand towards the bearded man. "This is Detective Sergeant Nixon," he said to Beasley.

"Hello," said Beasley.

"All right, John," Lyons said to Nixon.

Nixon took a step towards Beasley, holding a white envelope in his left hand. He took a pair of tweezers from his waistcoat pocket, inserted them into the envelope and produced the plastic sachet that had earlier contained a latchkey. At the bottom of the sachet was a layer of yellow powder.

"This is yours, I understand," Nixon said to Beasley.

"Is it fuck."

Nixon turned to Lyons.

Lyons said, "Tut, tut, tut," and raised his voice. "Bob."

Samuels came through the door. "What's up?"

"Show him your exhibit, John," Lyons said to Nixon.

Nixon raised the tweezers and Samuels stepped forward to examine it. "You seen this before?" said Nixon.

Samuels pointed at Beasley. "It's his."

"Bollocks."

"Watch your language," said Lyons.

"It's his all right," said Samuels. "I removed it from inside his underpants in the presence of Constable Lyons here while the prisoner was being searched."

"That's correct," said Lyons.

Nixon looked down at Beasley. "Do you want to tell us what this is?"

"I know what it is. It's a fit up."

Nixon replaced the plastic sachet inside the envelope. "My initial examination of this powder, that is by taste and smell, has given me cause to believe that it may be an illegal substance. It will now be sent away for forensic analysis. If, as I suspect, it is proved to be heroin or some other controlled drug, you will be charged with that offence. Do you understand?"

"It's double clear."

"You are not obliged to say anything but anything you do say will be taken down and may be used in evidence against you. Do you wish to say anything?"

"Get stuffed."

Nixon put the envelope into his inside pocket. "Charming."

"The prints, John," said Lyons.

"Yes," said Nixon. "I feel I ought to inform you that there's a good set of prints, fingerprints, on this packet. They appear to match your own."

"Sterling work," said Beasley.

"You understand what I'm saying?"

"Seeing as how Mr Nice Guy here has just had me handling the bloody thing, I've got a vague inkling of what you're on about."

"Bail, John," said Lyons.

Nixon looked at Samuels and raised his eyes towards the ceiling. "In view of your previous history, Mr Beasley, I don't think it would be in the public interest to grant bail until we've searched your premises or had a report back from the laboratory."

"Piss off, puppet."

"Watch it, sonny," said Nixon.

155

"Watch you? I'd need to be cross-eyed."

Nixon grinned and said to Lyons, "All right, Horace? Anything else?"

"That's fine, John."

Nixon walked to the door and opened it.

"Oh, John," said Lyons. "How much is there, do you reckon?"

"Less than half a gramme."

"Thanks again," said Lyons.

Nixon waved his hand and shut the door behind him.

"Looks open and shut to me," said Samuels, circling around behind Beasley.

"Afraid so," said Lyons. He placed his right foot on the table and began to untie the lace. "Unless we've made an awful mistake."

"What do you mean?" said Samuels.

Lyons tugged at the tongue of his shoe and eased it clear of his foot. "I'm trying to think back. We've been so busy today. Do you think it might be somebody else who had that packet?"

"I'd like to think that, Horace," said Samuels. "God knows, we all make the odd ricket. But what about the prints? Surely that will clear it up one way or the other."

Lyons massaged the inside of his toes through the sock. He nodded. "I was forgetting about the dabs."

Samuels put his hands on Beasley's shoulders. "That'll be the clincher. You can't argue with science. Pity." He patted Beasley's shoulders. "And he's been a good boy, too, hasn't he? Co-operative and everything? Maybe I should have a word with John. Tell him to hang fire for a while. Maybe even lose that packet. It's only half a gramme, he said. Obviously for personal use. Not a dealer, are you, Graham? Not one of those death pedlars we read about in the Sunday papers?"

Beasley moved his shoulders, trying to shrug Samuels' hands away. Samuels tightened his hold.

"Shame, really," said Samuels. "What do you think, Horace?"

Lyons rolled his sock half way off his foot and

156

scratched his instep. "That might be the best solution. The fairest. As you said, he could hardly be a dealer. Trouble is, Bob, Graham hasn't been all that co-operative. He can't really remember what happened in the pub and doesn't want to make a statement."

Samuels rocked Beasley back and fro by the shoulders. "Oh dear. He can't remember, eh? That is sad. But what about all those statements the cricketers made? Why not let him look at those, Horace? That might jog his memory. It might all come flooding back. We could be in for an epic."

Lyons removed his sock and held it up to his nose. "What a bouquet. Never mind the water torture, Bob, in future we'll give 'em the Lyons' sock." He dropped the sock into his shoe and used both hands to massage his toes. "Look at the statements? No, no, Bob, that's right out of order. No. Can't allow that. Judges' rules etcetera. No, we'll just have to hope that it all comes back to him. And I've got a feeling it might. He looks the intelligent sort to me. They often have good memories. So, listen, Bob. Why don't you nip along and have a word with John? Before he sends that stuff to the analyst. Just ask him to hold his horses for a while. You get that, Graham? Hold his horses."

"That's a good idea, Horace," said Samuels. He patted Beasley's shoulders. "I think Graham's had enough bad luck for one day."

Samuels moved to the door.

"Oh, and yes, Bob," said Lyons. "Drop that other package in, just in case."

"I'll get it now," said Samuels. He left the door open.

Lyons shook his sock and eased his toes into the opening. He looked up at Beasley. "You see, I'm trying to be reasonable."

"Sure."

"You sound discontented, Graham."

"Do I?"

"You don't know when you're well off."

"Aren't any of you straight?"

157

Lyons slipped his shoe back on and tied the lace. "I love this job, Graham. I really do. It's got everything. Ace wages, power, excitement, adventure, diversity. It's got everything. I can't understand anybody ever getting out of this game. Unless they're fucking dim enough to try and do it straight. You'd go mad in a month. It's impossible, son. Honesty's gone down the chute. The 'at it' attitude. Everybody's at it. The milkman's at it, the gas men are at it, the parson's probably at it, too. And you want us to play it straight? We'd be overwhelmed in a fortnight. You can only survive if you can get things done, Graham. And I'm getting Goff done. With you or without you that arrogant Mick is destined for the slammer. Got it?" He stood up and stamped his foot. "It's itching worse than ever now. You ever get that? Drives me crazy."

Samuels came through the open door and handed Lyons a brick-shaped package wrapped in jute. "I'll be upstairs, Horace."

"Thanks, Bob."

Samuels left, closing the door behind him.

"All right," said Lyons. "Let's get down to business. Are you ready to dicker, Graham?"

"You mean am I going to drop Goff in it."

Lyons yawned, tilting his head and rubbing both hands into his face. "You know, Graham, I never expected you to be so loyal."

"If Toaster's dead there'll have to be an inquest."

"True."

"It'll all come out."

"What will?"

"Police brutality."

Lyons pinched and pulled at the crutch of his trousers. "And who's going to make the accusations? Goff? Don't worry, he'll be sweet."

"Not with my help he won't."

Lyons sighed and drummed his fingers on the edge of the table. "Then you get done for the heroin."

"Stuff it."

"Oh, stuff it, eh? I think you're being a little hasty, Graham."

158

"Haven't we been through all this?"

"Not quite. You need help in adding up. You'll get the nine months suspended, won't you?"

"Maybe."

"No maybe about it. And then there's this new charge. A year on top, would you say?"

"I don't care."

"Well, I admire you, Graham. You're willing to swallow twenty-one months just to protect a man you've only met a few hours ago?"

"You never know. A decent brief. Might even get off."

Lyons stood up, knocking the chair into the wall. "You're fucking thick. Houdini couldn't get out of this." He walked around the table and across to the radiator. "Look. I gave you the good news. You can walk. Just give me the statement. But no. That's too much for you. You'd rather fuck me about. Well, you hear this, kid. You fuck Horace Lyons about and you don't get away with no poxy twenty-one months."

"What do you mean?"

"What do I mean? You come in here, drunk and disorderly, fighting in a pub, assaulting two police officers and you are found to be in possession of an illegal drug. That's serious, that is. In the morning, Mr Nixon will seek and be granted a warrant to search your premises. I personally will accompany him. And do you know what we will find at your place, Graham? Have you any idea?"

"No."

"What have you got hidden there?"

"Nothing."

Lyons walked back to the table, straightened the chair, sat down and dragged the jute-wrapped package towards himself. "Nothing, eh?" He tapped the package.

"What's that?" said Beasley.

"Something I'd hate to lose. There's eleven or twelve grammes in here, Graham. Worth a fortune. To me it's worth a fortune. To you it's worth five years. No one has eleven or twelve grammes for private use, Graham. Eleven or twelve grammes and you're a dealer. Get the idea now?"

"It won't wash."

Lyons laughed. "No?" He began to unwrap the package. "Come closer, Graham. I want you to take a good look at this gear. Get an expert opinion."

"I've seen enough."

Lyons unfolded three layers of jute wrapping from the package. He bent his head to blow scraps of lint from a plastic bag of powder. The bag was marked 'Barclays Bank. £5'.

"Look at that, Graham," he said. "Is that quality or is that quality?"

"I'm touching nothing."

Lyons massaged his scalp, clawing his hair towards his forehead. "I don't want you to touch it, you twerp. Just look at it. Imagine finding it at your gaff. Now, where's a good little hidey-hole."

"For God's sake."

Lyons stretched across the table and gripped Beasley's right wrist. "I'm just trying to show you an easy way out of this, son. And that's the truth."

Beasley wrenched his hand free, wiping it against his canvas jacket. "Fuck off. What would you know about truth?"

"Naughty, naughty," said Lyons, wagging his finger. He stood up and circled the table, leaning over Beasley. "The truth, Graham. I said it and I meant it. I give it to you and you throw it back in my face. Why's that now? Because it hasn't set you free." He slapped Beasley on the back. "You think it's a restricted commodity, do you? Precious? Hard to find? Well, if you ask me, Graham, there's too much of it about. It's everywhere, rearing its ugly head all round us. And you've got to be on your toes the whole time, ready to give it a whack, keep it down, bury it deep. Or it'll rise up and eat your heart out. It's a killer, Graham."

"You're full of shit."

Lyons stood upright and turned his body to lean against

the table. He crossed his legs, scratching at his left ankle with his right shoe. "Right, that's right. I am. And thank God for it. Yes, indeedy, that's the truth. I am full of shit. All these people cracking up, Graham, all the loonies in the boob, all the criers and moaners and nervous-breakdown cases, you know what their trouble is? Their real trouble? They're in trouble because they're running short of bullshit. They're overdosing on truth and bullshit's the only antidote."

Beasley shuffled his chair away from Lyons. "That's really deep that. Illuminating. You ought to be in advertising," said Beasley.

Lyons wriggled his little finger in his ear and looked at Beasley. He walked back around the table and sat down, tilting the chair against the wall. He flicked his little finger against his palm and probed his ear again. "Sarcasm is the slug of humour, didn't you know that? The refuge of morons."

"Sure."

Lyons rocked the chair forward onto its four legs and crouched into the table. "Illuminating."

"That's what I thought," said Beasley.

Lyons pushed the jute-wrapped package to the side of the table. "Try this for illumination. Imagine some poor innocent sod hauled into his local nick and fitted up something rotten. Maybe he took a pasting, too. Or he's got one to come. Imagine that's the truth, Graham. And imagine another truth. Imagine that out there in the big wide world are all these decent people, lawyers and writers and professors and social workers and ministers of the cloth. And imagine all these decent people – free and decent, Graham – imagine they're all deeply concerned about their fellow human beings and the need for us all to behave in a civilized manner. Imagine that's the truth. And then ask yourself this: how am I in this position and why am I so sure that nobody's going to do anything about it? And if you can come up with an answer that doesn't have that secret magic ingredient called bullshit then I'll eat your statement, drink the ink and shove the

161

pen up my arse. Because, Graham – and here's a touch of irony you're sure to enjoy – all those decent people out there going about their lawful business, free of physical restraint, all those people –"

He stopped as the door opened and Samuels leaned into the room, balancing his bodyweight on the handle.

"Sorry to interrupt, Horace," said Samuels. "Varley's here."

"Dick Varley?"

"Richard the lying heart," said Samuels.

"Why didn't you warn me?"

"Why don't I win the pools every week?"

"Christ," said Lyons. "Do you know what he wants?"

Samuels looked at Beasley and flicked his head backwards. Lyons threw the jute wrapping across the package and picked it up. He carried it out of the room, locking the door behind him.

Beasley took Lyons' cigarettes and matches from his pocket and lit one. He walked backwards and forwards the length of the room and sat on the radiator. He stubbed out the cigarette when he heard the key in the lock.

Lyons came back into the room, still holding the package, picking at his nose with his thumb. He sat down in his chair and dropped the package on the table. "Come and join me, Graham."

Beasley sat opposite him. "Who's Varley?"

"He's heavy brass from King Street and bad news for you, Graham. They want you down there, son. And unless you start writing, there won't be much I can do about it."

"What for?"

"What for what?"

"Why do they want me down there?"

"They've probably got a big pile of unsolveds they'd like to lay on you. They'll make you hold your hands up so high the papers'll be calling you Raffles. If you don't co-operate, I can't hold them off. Once you're down there, Graham, there'll be no deals. You'll be in more trouble than Jerry the Cat."

"Tom's the cat. Jerry's the mouse."

"Are we going to do business or not?"

"There's no need to shout."

Lyons picked up the jute-wrapped package, elbows on the table, balancing the package on the tips of his fingers. "What sort of flush you got on your bog?"

"Sorry?"

"The cistern. Chain or plunger?"

"On my bog?"

Lyons held the package in his right hand and moved it up and down through the air. "I was just wondering if that'd be a good place to find this."

Beasley leant back in his chair. "You're so smooth, you are. So subtle. Like a bee with one wing. I just can't keep up with you."

Lyons stood up and slapped the package onto the table, covering it with his hand. "I've been very patient with you, Graham. Very gentle. But all good things come to an end. Now what's it going to be?"

Beasley pushed his chair backwards, remaining seated. "I'll take the deep blue sea."

"You'll what?"

"Fuck your statement."

Lyons came up on his toes, leaning across the table. "Right, you little shit. Just listen –"

Beasley was standing, too, pushing his face at Lyons. "Listen? More bullshit. More earbashing –"

They both swung their heads towards the door as it opened. A uniformed Chief Superintendent looked at them through rimless glasses.

"Nice of you to knock, Dick," said Lyons.

Beasley sat down.

Varley nodded at Lyons. "Horace." He walked to the desk and looked down at Beasley. "You're Beasley, are you? Outside." He took off his hat and gestured towards the door.

Beasley stood up.

Lyons said, "Just a minute, Dick."

Varley walked back to the door and held it open. "I told you to get out," he said to Beasley.

163

Lyons shouted, "I said just a minute." He rounded the desk and stood between Beasley and the door. "He'll go when I fucking tell him to or he'll need a lot more help." He pushed Beasley in the chest. "Sit down."

Varley closed the door and stepped up to Lyons. "You're out of order, Horace. Right out of your box."

Lyons put both hands in his trouser pockets and pulled at his groin. "Just what sort of a cunt do you take me for, Chiefy?"

"Knock it off, Horace."

"Knock it off? You come in here to my nick, no courtesy, no warning, and start ordering my prisoners about. And you tell me to knock it off?"

"This is over your head."

"Over my head? And me with such a big one, according to you. The bloody Commissioner's not going to come in here and order my prisoners about."

"He's not your prisoner. He's been bailed."

"He's been bailed?"

"Please stop repeating everything I say."

Lyons moved his face close to Varley and lowered his voice. "You're well named, Clever Dick. But don't get flash with me. How can he be bailed?"

"Gently, Horace," said Varley, easing Lyons away with a hand on his chest. "You're out of focus. He was bailed at King Street."

"But he's here. His details are here. His property's here. His body's here. How can he be bailed at King Street?"

"All the details are on the computer. It was decided to give him bail. I'm just here to see it goes smoothly. Osborne's outside."

"That creepy brief? I've rowed him out of here once today."

"Presumably that's why he went to King Street and why they sent me back with him."

Lyons scratched at his right armpit and picked his nose. "And you gave him bail without reference to us? No, no, no, no. What the hell is going on?"

Varley looked down at his hat. He twirled the rim

around one finger and caught it by the peak. "What do you think's going on? Why don't you ask Halliday?"

"You mean he's buying his way out?"

"For Heaven's sake, Horace," said Varley, his eyes sliding towards Beasley.

Lyons turned to look at Beasley. "How do you know Osborne?"

"I've never heard of him," said Beasley.

Lyons swung back to Varley. "Oh yeah?"

Varley placed his hat on his head, fluting the sides and top. "Maybe it's the other one."

"Yeah," said Lyons. "Yeah," nodding his head, putting his hands back in his pocket. "The mystery man. How much?"

Varley stepped between Lyons and Beasley. "All this can be sorted out later, Horace. There's one or two things you don't know about."

Lyons moved wide of Varley to get a view of Beasley. "I don't know about? And what about you? Do you know what that bastard – Goff, whose prints we still ain't got, who might be Lord Lucan for all the fuck we know – do you know what that bastard did to the Oaf? I was here, Richard. He's been fucking maimed."

"There was an exchange of discourtesies, I understand."

"You what? For fuck's sake."

Varley moved his head towards the door. "Can't we discuss this privately, Horace?"

"Aaggh." Lyons waved his hand across the front of his face. "I just can't believe this."

"Suit yourself then," said Varley. "The Oaf's been squared. He won't welcome your objections. It's what he wants. A little sweetener."

"Little sweetener."

"Not so little perhaps. There'll be no complaints so it's no good taking it personally. They're bailed, Horace, and that's the end of it. Take it up with Halliday if you like."

"I'd rather talk to a fresh turd," said Lyons. He sat on the table and rubbed his hands up and down his thighs, from knee to crotch. "At least you must know who he is."

"Who?"

"Jesus."

"You mean Goff? Well, somebody does."

"He's not a mystery?"

"Mystery? What do I know? He's got the brief, he's got the bread, he's got the bail. Leave it there, man."

"I've got a feeling about him."

"You've got a prejudice, Horace, which we all try to overlook."

Lyons pushed himself away from the table and stood in front of Beasley. He jerked his thumb at Varley. "This brassed-up fart used to be a good copper."

Varley clapped his hands and rubbed them together. "The last time we had a ruck you called me a whited sepulchre. I looked it up. It gave me a good laugh."

Lyons spat on the floor in front of Varley.

"You don't know when to stop, do you?" said Varley.

"Here, you can have him," said Lyons. He turned and took Beasley by the ear, twisting and lifting. "Get the fuck out of my sight."

Beasley slashed at Lyons' arm, knocking it away. "Keep your filthy hands to yourself," said Beasley.

Lyons paled, his mouth slackened, his eyes stretched and bulged. He rushed at Beasley, driving him back to the far wall, his left elbow at Beasley's throat, hacking at him with his right fist.

Varley shouted, "Samuels, Samuels," and looped an arm around Lyons' neck. "Cool it, Horace, cool it."

"You little snot-nosed cunt," Lyons screamed at Beasley. He brought his knee up between Beasley's legs and continued punching at him with his right hand. His bottom lip was foaming with spittle.

Varley levered Lyons' head away from Beasley. Samuels came running into the room and dragged Beasley clear of the two officers. Varley pushed Lyons forward across the radiator. "Get him out of here," he said to Samuels.

166

"Come on," said Samuels, guiding Beasley towards the door.

Lyons, pinned across the radiator, allowed his body to relax. "I'm all right now, Richard," he said.

"That's good, Horace," said Varley, keeping his grip. He looked over his shoulder. "Get him to sign a bail form, give him his property and kick him into the rain. Move it."

"Ease up, Dick," said Lyons.

"In a minute, Horace."

Lyons twisted his head towards the door. "You enjoy yourself, Graham," he shouted. "Remember that little plastic packet. I'll be around to see you soon."

Samuels pushed Beasley through the door and slammed it shut. He was smiling. "You're a right little stirrer, aren't you," he said to Beasley.

"He's disgusting," said Beasley.

"Come on," said Samuels. He took Beasley by the elbow and escorted him back into the charge room and through the counter flap. Samuels stayed on the other side of the counter. He gave Beasley a bail form and a pen. "Sign that while I get your gear."

Samuels carried a chair to the lockers at the side of the room and stood on the chair as he rummaged through the cartons.

Beasley signed the form and called, "How's Goff?"

"Your mate? The fee-fi-fo-fum merchant? A game lad that. I'll get a lot of mileage out of him," said Samuels. He pulled a bag half out of the locker and examined the tag. He pushed it back and drew another. "Six fucking bags in here and naturally yours is the last one I get my mitts on. Ain't there a name for that?"

"Is there?"

"Murphy's Law I think they call it. Thought you'd know that. Here it is."

Samuels shut the locker, replaced the chair and carried the bag to the counter. "Beasley, Graham. That's you, ain't it?"

"I'm not Irish," said Beasley.

Samuels handed him the bag. "Just check the seal."

Beasley picked up the bag. "It looks okay. Did you hear what I said? I said I'm not Irish."

Samuels took the bag and cut the seal. "You don't look it, you don't sound it, but you know what they say about lying down with dogs."

"No, I don't."

Samuels emptied the contents of the bag onto the counter. "They say you get fleas."

"Oh," said Beasley. "Is that right? Do you mean I'll be eating out of a trough tonight?"

"Mmm?"

"Does that mean I'll be grunting through a snout and grow a little curly tail?"

Samuels laughed. "All right, all right." He took a clipboard from under the counter. "Horace been giving you a bad time, has he?"

"You know what he was doing."

Samuels marked his place on the clipboard with a pen and laid it aside. He folded his arms and leant on the counter. "He's a little paranoid at times, is Horace. Specially when he hears a Mick accent."

"I said I wasn't Irish."

"Yeah, but he wasn't after you, was he?"

"How is Goff?"

"He looked in good shape, all things considered. Varley and the brief had him wheeled out of here while you were chatting with Horace."

"Chatting?"

"Well, it's all part of the game, son, all part of the game."

"The brief went with him, did he?"

"That's right. In a private ambulance. Blue lights flashing, men in white coats, big red cross on a big low limo. Just like a film it was. Gave us all quite a turn. Now, let's get the paperwork sorted. You've signed the bail form? Good. Just pick up the items as I tick them off, all right? Bunch of keys, five keys."

Beasley picked up the keys and put them in his pocket. "No message?"

"One steel comb. Message? From Osborne? He only speaks to money, son. And I don't think you fit that description. One steel comb. Come on!"

Beasley took the comb. "I meant from Goff."

Samuels tapped his pen against the clipboard. "Now when I said he was all right, I didn't mean he was drinking champagne. He wasn't all that articulate, as they say. They done a nasty job on his knees. Still, he was nowhere near cowed. Kept asking about your other mate, what's-his-name. One packet of Silk Cut containing four cigarettes."

"Toaster."

"Yeah, Toaster. No one been nicking your fags, have they? Terrible bunch of villains in here."

"How did he take that?" said Beasley.

"How did he take what?"

"About Toaster?"

"What about him?"

Beasley took Lyons' cigarettes and matches from his pocket and placed them on the counter. "Have you heard anything about Toaster?"

"What's wrong with you?" said Samuels.

"Horace said he's copped it."

"Who?"

"Toaster. Horace said he was dead."

Samuels put the clipboard on the counter and trapped it under his elbow. "No, that's rubbish. Brace up now. Take no notice of that. He's all right. Your mate, Toaster? Released hours ago. Honest. Horace was just trying to soften you up, isolate you. It's an old stroke. Told you he had a dodgy heart, didn't he? A regular set-piece with Horace, that. Hey, not so quick. One Bic lighter."

Beasley flicked flame to one of his own cigarettes. "The bastard," he said.

"One handkerchief. I don't know why they didn't let you keep that."

"What a bastard."

"Try to forget it. He wanted a statement, didn't he? He'll do anything to get a statement."

"A twenty-four carat bastard," said Beasley. He reached out to pick up his wallet.

Samuels rapped him on the knuckles with his pen. "Wait till I tick it off. One wallet, assorted papers. You can take it now. One pocket diary. That Horace, he ain't so bad, you know. Plenty of friends upstairs, a lot of pull, but never abuses it, know what I mean? Normally, very, very steady. But now and then he gets a bee in his bonnet. Your mate Goff was more like a hive. D'you understand?"

"Sure."

"I mean, he's a good bloke most of the time. That's straight. A bit sensitive about being made a cunt of. And he thought your mate was making a cunt of him. That's what this drama's been all about."

"Sure."

Samuels relaxed against the counter, clicking the top of his pen. "He had us all jangled up here. He figured some sort of heavy mob were going to come storming in on a rescue mission. Wouldn't ask for help, of course. Not Horace. Same thing. Frightened of making a cunt of himself. One packet of fruit gums. Oh, yeah. And we're keeping your penknife. Blade was black, Graham. Got to check it out. Here's a receipt. Okay. Let's do the money. Eighteen pence in change. Three oncers, two fivers. That right?"

"What do you mean, the blade was black?"

"It's just routine. Dope check. Never comes to anything. Is the money all right?"

"Sure."

"Good. Sign here."

At the top of the police-station steps, Beasley stopped and turned towards the car park. A man carrying an umbrella ran through the rain.

"Graham, Graham, are you all right?" he called, one foot on the bottom step.

Beasley looked over his shoulder and threw away his cigarette. "I guessed it was you when Horace said there was a creepy brief outside."

"Oh," said Osborne. "Did you? How endearing."

"What's the latest on the others, Goff and Toaster?"

Osborne climbed the steps two at a time, closing the umbrella as he reached the porch. "Tom'll mend quickly enough once his knees have been treated. I haven't seen the other chap. He has been discharged, however, so it can't be serious. I understand he's staying with his girlfriend. But what about yourself? Don't you have an overcoat?"

"I left it somewhere. I'll get it tomorrow."

"Are you sure you're all right?"

"Well, I'm out."

"Yes. Look. May I offer you a lift?"

"Not tonight, John. Anyway, I live near here."

Osborne turned, sweeping his umbrella in an arc towards the street. "I don't think it's going to stop."

"I like the rain."

"Yes, so do I. But without an overcoat?"

"I'll be okay."

Osborne trailed the tip of the umbrella along a gully in the flagstones. "It's entirely up to you, of course. But could you spare a few moments. A brief chat?"

"Chat?"

"Perhaps the car?"

"No moves, John, all right?"

"Graham, this is business."

Osborne held the umbrella above Beasley's head as they walked through the car park. He opened the passenger door for Beasley and shook and folded the umbrella before taking the driver's seat himself. He dropped the umbrella on the floor behind his seat.

Beasley picked up a bowler hat that was lying on the dashboard and placed it on his head. "And the snow's all gone."

"Please, Graham," said Osborne, removing the hat. "It's been raining for hours." He tossed the hat onto the back seat. "How did it go in there?"

"I didn't make a statement if that's what's worrying you."

"No? You gave them nothing in writing? That's always wise."

"They're ready to fit me up, though. They tricked me into handling a bag of snort."

"Typical. But I shouldn't be too concerned about that."

"I'm sure you shouldn't. I bet you've got different fingerprints."

Osborne sighed and rubbed a gloved hand against the windscreen. "I think you know what I meant. Have you still got my home number?"

"Come on," said Beasley.

Osborne removed the glove from his right hand and took out a wallet from his inside pocket. "Here's my card," he said. "I'm putting my home number on the bottom." He wrote on the card with a gold-coloured pen and gave it to Beasley.

Beasley slanted the card into the light. "John V. Osborne. What's the V stand for?"

"Victor."

"That's nice. And I've got nothing to worry about?"

"Not from the police."

"Because of all that money that's been handed around?"

Osborne slapped his loose glove against the steering wheel. "What money?"

"Leave it out, John. Horace and that heavy-braid number, Varley. They had a barney about it."

"I know nothing about money," said Osborne.

"Sure," said Beasley. "You charmed us out."

"You can thank Tom's friend Jacko for your early release. He arrived at the pub at the same time as the police. He wisely waited outside and questioned some of the customers who were allowed to leave. He saw you being carried out and followed. I was here thirty minutes behind you and Goff. And a colleague arranged for Toaster's discharge. All quite legal and above board, Graham."

"Sure, sure," said Beasley. "The law couldn't wait to get rid of us."

Osborne turned in his seat until he was facing Beasley. "I fear I'm going to have to be indiscreet with you, Graham."

"Really?" said Beasley. "That sounds nice." He put the card into his top pocket and offered Osborne a cigarette. Osborne held up his hand in refusal and flipped the ashtray out of the dashboard.

"Bear with me a moment," Osborne said. "Tom tells me I've met this Toaster chappie. But I can't place him."

Beasley lit his cigarette with the Bic lighter. "Tall, about my age, always smiling, long fair hair. Carries a brush around with him. Fantastic dimples."

"Oh, yes," said Osborne. "A little slow at the bar."

Beasley clicked the lighter on and off, on and off. "That's mint, that is. That's all you can remember is it? That he's a bit of a beer burglar?"

"No, no. It was the hairbrush that brought it back. They were teasing him about the other thing."

Beasley put the lighter into his pocket. "He is a bit tight, as it happens. But a lot of good blokes are like that. They can't help it. Like bad skin or crooked teeth. Doesn't mean a thing."

"Yes. Perhaps. The point is, however, that he is one of Goff's people. Whereas you, Graham, well, you're the surprise of the year."

"What do you mean, one of Goff's people?"

Osborne swished the glove against the steering wheel. "This is the area of indiscretion I was talking about. Have you any idea of who he is and what he does?"

"Aah," said Beasley, tapping Osborne on the forearm. "I've got it now. Shock-horror time for you, was it, when a little nobody like Beasley appeared on those steps?"

"Not quite," said Osborne. "I took the opportunity — perhaps you might think the liberty — of looking you over in your cell. You were squirming in your sleep."

"Squirming? That's a bit crude, Ossie."

Osborne looped the glove across the steering wheel and flicked at the empty fingers. "Yes. Well, writhing then. You were writhing in your sleep."

Beasley stabbed his cigarette into the ashtray, breaking it in two, losing the burning tip and grinding it into the carpet with his foot. "You were embarrassed then, were you, seeing an old acquaintance, an old and low acquaintance, in such exalted company?"

"I do wish you'd stop it, Graham. This is very difficult for me," said Osborne. He tapped his fingernail against his teeth. "I wasn't embarrassed at all, not in the slightest. I was frightened."

"For me?"

"Yes, for you."

"Well, well. Fair enough, Ossie. But I'm out now."

"Oh, you're such a fool," said Osborne. "Do you really think it's ended? How well do you know Tom?"

"I met him for the first time today."

"God."

"He was drinking with Toaster. Me and Toaster are old mates. And don't call me a fool, John. I know who Tom Goff is. He's a villain. A serious villain. And a clever one too. Toaster says he's never even had a parking ticket."

"A clever villain."

174

"That's what I've heard," said Beasley. "And a man with a lot of balls. That's what I know. That Tom could outstare God."

Osborne exhaled a heavy breath and pursed his lips. He took off his other glove and draped it with its twin across the rim of the steering wheel. He rubbed his eyes and cheekbones with both hands. "Graham, please listen. Tom Goff is not some modern-day Al Capone with a black belt in dirty looks. Tom Goff is the most dangerous person I've ever met in my life. And I've known him for seventeen years, Graham. Not a day."

"I know he's dangerous," said Beasley. "I've seen him in action. So does the Oaf."

"Graham, Graham. I'm not talking about big and strong and quick and deadly. I'm not talking about that sort of dangerous. Tom's got a dangerous mind, a dangerous way of thinking. Do you know what 'hubris' is, Graham. Hubris?"

"No."

"It's a Greek word. It means inordinate pride. Overweening, insolent pride. When I first met Tom I was working for the Lasser brothers. Do you remember them? They were Turkish Cypriots, very big in the early sixties, clubs, cheap hotels, pornography. They were tough boys, frightened of nobody but not reckless, always ready to talk. One of Tom's people had opened up a place in Praed Street and they arranged a meeting with Tom to complain about it. And they asked me to come along to show how respectable they were. They didn't want to fight, they wanted to negotiate and I was to be on hand to draw up an agreement. They were willing to pay this man, Dwyer I think his name was, to close down and leave them in peace. They thought he was giving the area a bad name. And they explained all this to Tom, careful to be polite. When they'd finished he said, 'I rob money lorries' and just walked out. Frank Lasser looked at his brother and said, 'Hubris', and they both shrugged. It was something I didn't understand at the time but they realized only too well what he was saying. He was telling them they were shit."

"I rob money lorries," repeated Beasley, smiling.

"Yes. That was the only thing he said during the whole conversation."

"And what happened?"

"Oh, in a way that was rather typical too. The Lassers made a mistake. They interfered with Dwyer's family. His nine-year-old son, as I remember. The response was overwhelming. Bodies everywhere. Club managers, doormen, croupiers. Five or six within a matter of weeks. The Lassers sold up and went home. Tom told me later that if only they'd settled for bombing Dwyer out or burning down his shop, he would never have interfered. You know what a prude he is about dirty books and topless barmaids. Or, then again, perhaps you don't."

Beasley lit a cigarette and stared at the lighter flame. "How come you went to work for him?"

"He asked me to."

"But you thought he was dangerous."

"Graham, I know he's dangerous. I was frightened to refuse. He knows well enough a lawyer's duties to his client. Duties which I'm now failing to uphold."

Beasley turned his head to look at Osborne. "By telling me, you mean? Yeah, and very interesting too, Ossie. But it's not like you. So what's it all about?"

Osborne put his hand on Beasley's arm. "Hubris, Graham, hubris. Nobody in the world is going to break Tom Goff's knees and hear no more about it. There's going to be a bloodbath, Graham. Believe me. I know it. I want you to leave the country for three or four months until it's all over. I'll even lend you the money. I want you to go somewhere that will provide a first-class alibi, where you can keep up a high profile."

"What are you telling me?" said Beasley. "He's going to take on the law?"

Osborne grunted. "The law's a meaningless concept to Tom. They're just people who hurt him. He'll make a violent response. No doubt, absolutely no doubt. You'll be in very serious trouble, Graham. They'll be looking for everybody with a grudge against the people he hurts in return."

"What about Toaster?"

"Don't be naive, Graham. Toaster's one of his people."

"I went to school with Toaster."

"Somebody went to school with Jack the Ripper."

"Give me a minute, John, please. Let me think this out."

Beasley stretched his head back over the seat, looking up at the roof of the car, letting the smoke trickle from his mouth. He moved his head towards the police station. "You know about the dungeon in there?"

Osborne rolled his right glove back onto his hand, easing it down between the joints. "Yes. They say it was built for Rudolph Hess during the last war."

"Is that right? What was wrong with a good plastic surgeon and a safe seat in the shires?"

Osborne wriggled the fingers of his left hand into his glove. "You're not going to become tiresome about class distinctions, are you, Graham?"

"Hey, hey," said Beasley. "Don't get ratty. I liked that bit with the umbrella, John. When we were walking to the car. Manners maketh middle-class man."

"Oh dear."

Beasley drew smoke into his mouth and out through his nose. He sat up and stubbed the cigarette into the ashtray. "Something happened in there," he said.

"So I understand," said Osborne.

"No, to me."

"Ahh."

"Tom tell you how he nicked the truncheon?"

"And assaulted Inspector Grace a second time? Yes. He was proud of that."

Beasley took the cigarette packet from his pocket. "Terrible Tom," he said. "Tattooing on the bars with his stolen stick. But they were ready-eyed the second time. Lances, shields, tactics all worked out. Their lips were still moving."

The last cigarette spilled through his fingers and rolled to the floor of the car. Beasley screwed the packet into a ball and threw it down, stamping on it with his foot. "Fucking cancer anyway."

Osborne picked up the cigarette and rolled it across the tips of his fingers, straightening the creases. He tapped it against the steering wheel and handed it to Beasley.

"Thanks," said Beasley. "They were frightened, see? Monsters but frightened. You could have recharged a battery with what was flying about down there. He had no chance this time, even with the truncheon. Except for one little moment."

Beasley took his lighter from his pocket and lit the cigarette.

"One little moment. That was when a stick flew loose and landed right in front of me. And Goff turned around, his hand reaching for the stick and them holding his legs against the bars. For a moment there, everything stopped. Nothing. Heavy breathing. I heard the heavy breathing and noticed that grey colour people get when they're really wound up. And they're all looking at me and the stick. It was like something out of the Bible, that stick. It was ready to crack the world asunder. It glowed, it was alive. Then the sergeant shouted. He was shouting at me. He wanted his stick back. And I picked it up and threw it across the cell, away from everyone, and that's when they all started again."

Osborne handed Beasley his handkerchief. "Here, wipe your face. You're sweating."

Beasley took the handkerchief, balling it between the palms of his hands. "Listen. Afterwards, when I'd been moved to that other cell, this Welsh cunt, cement-head, he comes in and puts the boot in a couple of times."

"Who was that?"

"Davis. That don't matter. He puts the boot in and the sergeant, Swakely, he stops him. 'He threw your stick away,' says the Welsh toe-rag. 'Yes,' says the sergeant. 'But he could have given it to his mate.' Do you know what I mean, John, do you know what I'm saying?"

"What?"

"I'd been feeling a bit clever about that stick, my little flash of courage, my bit of defiance. It had never occurred to me to give that stick to Goff. It wasn't just that I didn't have the guts, I didn't even have the thought. Do you understand that, John?"

"Relax, Graham, relax."

"Fuck relax. Do you understand what I'm saying? Do you get it?"

Osborne bent forward and turned on the radio. "It's plain enough, Graham. Shouting won't make it any clearer."

"What are you doing?"

"Giving us some music."

"What? What for?"

"Some people find it soothing. I'm hoping to save my handkerchief."

Beasley looked at the handkerchief and laughed. He began to fold it. "Christ, I'm sorry."

"Careful with that cigarette," said Osborne.

Beasley squashed the cigarette into the ashtray and closed it. He handed the handkerchief to Osborne.

"He thinks I'm shit. He thinks you're shit," said Osborne. "At the bottom line, we're all shit. That's how his head works."

"No," said Beasley. "You're wrong. He pulled me up on that. You're wrong, John. You don't know it all."

"I was in the country with him once," said Osborne. "We were going to buy this house, near Sevenoaks. The owners, very smart, very wealthy, were showing us over the property. They had this guard dog, a huge German brute, I forget the breed, but ferocious. It was bothering Marion, that's Tom's wife. Perhaps it was her period. It kept nuzzling up to her. So he gave it a rap. This was an animal a normal person wouldn't dare to look at and he backhanded it across the nose. The dog bit him, nothing too serious, a nip on the thigh. The owners were mortified. The dog drew back, snarling. Tom was outraged. He leapt on the dog, wrestled it to the ground, punched and kneed it into stupidity and then stretched its jaws back until they snapped. He was covered in blood, the dog had got in a couple of more serious bites, and his suit was a mess of blood, saliva, mud and urine. Marion and the other woman, the owner's wife, were hysterical. The owner was on his knees by the dead dog, tears streaming down his cheeks, and he looked up at Tom and said, 'Why? Why?' Tom looked down at this poor, broken beast, its mouth slack and distorted, the top teeth sagging down below the bottom, and he said, 'What do you mean why? He bit me. Where can I clean up?' It would have chilled you to see it, Graham.''

"Sure, sure."

"I'm telling you."

"Hey," said Beasley, his voice rising. "I'm telling you something, John. I'm not going anywhere, you know. I think I'll hang around. Maybe I'm waking my head up again. I've been thinking about that for a couple of hours now. I mean I've been feeling a cunt for a couple of hours. Why? Because I acted like a cunt and I've got to face up to it. But facing something, knowing something, that doesn't cure it. Just because you know that when you think a certain way you're thinking like a cunt, that knowledge doesn't stop you thinking that way. I mean, you can be acting like a cunt and knowing it and keep on doing it because if you stop you think it's going to hurt even more. Well, I've had enough of that, John. I'll take Goff, hubris, humbug and all the dead dogs you can dig up."

Osborne blew through his mouth, fluting the fingers of his gloved left hand along his bottom lip.

"What does that mean?" said Beasley.

"It's a middle-class raspberry," said Osborne.

Beasley poked Osborne on the thigh with his index finger. "That tale about the dog. It would have been better if you'd made it a poodle or a Jack Russell. Better from your point of view, I mean."

"Poodle, parrot, piranha fish, what's it matter? The man thinks he's above nature," said Osborne. He patted his hair. "I should know better. My advice has been systematically rejected for twenty-five years and yet I still feel aggrieved."

Beasley smiled. "Come on, John, don't be like that. I really appreciate the loan of your ear. After a double helping of Horace's Friday-night philosophy, it's a pleasure to talk to someone who lets you get a word in edgeways."

"What will you do?"

"I'll leave it a couple of days. Then I'll go and see Toaster. Let him know I'm available."

"I meant now. It's still raining."

"Yeah. Maybe I'll get a hamburger or something and go to bed."

"Why don't you come to my place? It's warm and comfortable. I can offer you a hot drink and something to eat."

"Thee and sympathy."

"What do you say? A little spliff and I'll run you back whenever you like."

"No travel brochures."

"No travel brochures. Cross my heart," said Osborne.

"Do we pass a tobacconist on the way? I could smoke a firework."

"I'll make sure we do," said Osborne, clipping his seatbelt into its socket. He reached forward and started the engine. The car moved, its headlights fracturing the puddles.

"To Victor the spoils," said Beasley.

"What was that?" said Osborne, turning to look at him.

Beasley, the seatbelt pulled across his chest, was peering through the side window at the police station. The reflection from the blue lamp shimmered and died on the wet concrete steps.

Goff swivelled in the seat and lifted the carrier bag onto his lap. Beasley opened his eyes. "What is it?"

Goff folded the sacking and stuffed it into the side pocket of his tracksuit. He lifted the gun from the bag and balanced it across his knees. He rolled the bag into a ball and jammed it down on top of the sacking. He zipped the pocket closed.

Toaster touched Beasley on the shoulder. "Crisis time."

"What happened to those famous ears of yours?" said Goff.

Beasley hunched towards the windscreen. Three men were leaving the club. "Sergeants Swakely and Kilbride," he said.

"And a dwarf," said Toaster. "How the hell did he get into the police force?"

"He was bigger than that," said Beasley. "No, that can't be him. He's not the one. He can't be law, Tom."

Goff folded back the stock, primed the gun and eased it along his arm. "He's unlucky then."

"Shit, Tom, he must be a civilian."

"Don't start Tomming me now."

"They're all as pissed as rats," said Toaster.

Goff combed the helmet mask down across his chin with his left hand. "Cover your faces. I'll get out first and put them against the car. Toaster, you go in and pat them down. If there's any trouble, get well clear as fast as you can. Graham, if he gets tangled up with them, then we go in and help. Otherwise, I don't want you near them. Keep it simple. And both of you. Stay well the life side of me."

Toaster lowered the mask across his face. "He's right, though, Tom. They just don't have blue midgets."

Goff swung sideways, slapping the dashboard with his left hand. "Now look. I don't give a tinker's curse if that's the bearded lady out there. Those two are going. And whoever's in their company has to go too. I can do this myself and I'm beginning to wish I had. If you've got any doubts, take off. Just don't do it in the other motor."

Toaster stretched past Beasley to grip Goff's shoulder. He rocked him to and fro. "Hey, hey, hey," he said. "Cut it out, Tom, cut it out. No one's running anywhere. Let's have no more of that talk."

"All right," said Goff. He pushed Toaster's hand away and turned to look through the windscreen. "Let's have no more of that frigging right-and-wrong talk either. This is far too important for that."

Beasley stifled a laugh by coughing into his hand.

Goff looked at him. "If you're with us, cover your face."

Beasley lowered his mask.

"What's he doing?" said Toaster, staring through the windscreen.

One of the men had broken away from the others and was rooting at the raised flowerbeds that lined the top end of the car park.

"That's Kilbride," said Beasley.

"He's snatching the daffs."

"No, look. He's eating them."

Kilbride came away from the flowerbeds with bunches of daffodils in both hands. He was eating the heads.

"As last meals go, that wouldn't be a bad one," said Toaster.

Kilbride ran to catch the other two men and began beating at their heads with the daffodil stalks.

"That's near enough," said Goff. He slid open the door and stepped down onto the tarmac. He walked towards the three men, holding the gun parallel to his right leg. He stopped on the fringe of the lamplight.

Sergeant Swakely saw him first and pushed the others

183

away from him. "Is that you, Rollo?" Swakely called to Goff.

Goff lifted the gun to firing height and pointed it at Swakely.

"Who is it, Arthur?" said the small man.

"Shut up, Sammy," said Swakely. "Is this another of your fucking stunts, Rollo?"

"That ain't Rollo," said Kilbride. "Not unless he's wearing stilts."

Goff, supporting the barrel of the gun with his left hand, said, "All of you, over by the car. You, Stumpy, you take the bonnet."

"What did he call me?" said Sammy.

Swakely held up both hands, palms spread. "Let's all stay nice and calm."

"That's one ugly hole. That's the ugliest fucking hole I've ever seen," said Kilbride.

"Nice and calm," repeated Swakely.

Kilbride let the daffodil stalks in his left hand fall to the ground. He held up the bunch in his right hand and walked towards Goff. "Peace, brother," he said. "We come in peace."

Toaster stepped out of the gloom on Goff's left. Kilbride saw him and halted, squinting his eyes. "There's two of them, Arthur," he called back to Swakely.

"Three," said Swakely.

"It's one of our shooters, one of the specials," shouted Kilbride.

Swakely took a step forward. "Get back here, Will. Do as they tell you."

Kilbride moved away from the gun, crabwise towards Toaster. "I'm a bobby, son," he said. "An officer of the law. See this?" He lifted his left leg and plucked at the blue serge of his trousers. "Regulation strides. Look at these boots. Let me show you my ID."

"Get him over to the car," said Goff.

Toaster advanced on Kilbride and stabbed his fingers into his shoulder.

Kilbride stumbled away from him, dropping the daf-

184

fodil stalks. "Easy, easy, easy," he said.

"Get over to the car," said Toaster.

Kilbride stood straight, tugging at the back of his brown tweed jacket. "If you're going to be like that, I'd just as soon go home."

Toaster placed his left hand around the back of Kilbride's neck. "Try an act of contrition, Will," he said. "A perfect act of contrition."

"Say again."

"It's forever for you, Will."

"Come on," said Goff.

Toaster drove his right fist into Kilbride's stomach. Kilbride lurched forward, grunting. Toaster spun him around, slipping his hand inside Kilbride's coat and snatching the truncheon from Kilbride's trouser pocket. He kept Kilbride off-balance, propelling him past Swakely and Sammy. Kilbride stumbled against the car, fell across the bonnet and sank to his knees. Toaster thrust the truncheon into the side pocket of his dungarees and loomed over Kilbride, patting him down.

"No," called Goff. "Get them all there first."

Toaster backed away from the car, moving around to Goff in a wide arc.

Kilbride looked over his shoulder at Sergeant Swakely. "They're going to do us in, Arthur. They're going to do us in." He turned his head, crawled to the front wheel and began to vomit over the edge of the bumper bar.

Goff tilted the gun at Swakely and Sammy. "You two, get over there with him. Drape yourselves across the car."

Swakely put his right hand on Sammy's shoulder. "This is Sammy Skeed," he said. "A professional dancer. He's got nothing to do with this."

"How would you know?" said Goff.

"I've got a good memory."

"Too good, maybe. Over by the car."

Swakely ran his right hand up and down his face, massaging his cheekbone. "I'm telling you the truth. Years ago I used to dabble a bit myself. Me and Sammy, we worked together. He's just a dancer. No, I don't mean that. Another few inches and he'd have been up there with Kelly and Astaire, wouldn't you, Sammy?"

"Whatever you say, Arthur."

"We met by chance tonight and had a drink to celebrate old times. Sheer chance. Over there," Swakely jerked his thumb behind him, at the nightclub.

"The car," said Goff.

"Let him go," said Sergeant Swakely.

"I won't tell you again."

Swakely sighed and buttoned up his blazer. He lifted his elbows and sawed them backwards and forwards. "You want to dance, Sammy?"

"What's going on, Arthur?" said Sammy.

"They want to see you move."

"I don't think so, Arthur."

"Trust me," said Swakely. "You remember Shadow?"

"This is crazy."

Swakely swung away from Sammy and bowed. "Gentlemen, your indulgence, please." He smiled at Goff. "My last performance."

Toaster stepped closer to Goff. "What the hell are you doing, Tom?" he whispered.

"Admiring his gall."

"But what if someone comes out?"

"Then the curtain comes down."

Sammy looked up at the lamp-post. "This light's no good." He tapped his feet on the ground. "There's no return, Arthur, no return."

"For fuck's sake, Sammy," said Swakely. "Just cue me in."

Sammy bit his bottom lip and looked towards Goff and Toaster. He faced Swakely, clicking his fingers, counting. "And a one, and a two, and a three."

Swakely lowered his head. "I'm getting it. Once more, Sammy."

Sammy clicked and counted.

"Okay," said Swakely, eyes half-closed. "I've got it now."

"The short version, Arthur," said Sammy. "Let's keep it tight."

Swakely sang, creaking into the tune, stumbling for pitch and timing.

> Shades of night are falling and I'm lonely
> Standing on the corner feeling blue

"An accolade to abuse," said Toaster out of the corner of his mouth.
"Quiet," said Goff.

> Sweethearts out for fun pass me one by one

Behind Swakely, Sammy dipped in and out of view, humming harmony and clicking his fingers.

> Guess I'll wind up like I always do

Swakely began to dance, his rubber heels squeaking, shuffle and tap, shuffle and tap, arms taut over his hips, hands splayed, big teeth gleaming.

> Me and my shadow
> Strolling down the avenue
> Just me and my shadow
> And not a soul to tell our troubles to

Sammy glided to the edge of the lamplight, a blur of yellow and black. He swayed and whirled, lithe and fluent, twisting, soaring. His feet tattooed the tarmac. He moved in a semi-circle, flirting with light and shade, his arms flashing. Swakely, dipping his knees, sang on.

> And when it's twelve o'clock we climb the stairs
> We never knock for no one's there
> Just me and my shadow
> All alone and feeling blue

Sammy danced around the car, hands pumping, feet slapping. Kilbride, glossy yellow petals smearing his chin, turned to look.

> Me and my shadow
> Strolling down the avenue

Sammy slowed, easing back towards the lamp, letting his feet wind down into Swakely's closing chorus.

> Just me and my shadow
> All alone and feeling blue

The silence was broken by Beasley's clapping, the sound muffled by his gloves.

Swakely dropped his arms. Grinning and sweating, he turned to Sammy and picked him up in a bear-hug.

Sammy, whooping and laughing and gasping for air, his feet off the ground, slapped Swakely on the back. "You were marvellous, Arthur. Fucking marvellous."

"King Sammy," said Swakely. "King Sammy." He swung around to Goff. "I told you he was a dancer." His hands slid to his knees, bracing his back. He was panting.

"Incandescent," said Toaster. "You'd stop dying to see it."

Sergeant Swakely straightened his back and took hold of Sammy again, speaking into his ear and pushing him towards the car-park exit. Sammy started to move away and then stopped, looking from Swakely to Goff.

"I told him he could go now," said Swakely.

Goff made a noise in his throat, turned his head, lifted his mask above his mouth and spat. He turned back to Swakely and jerked the gun towards the car. "Take him in the motor," he said. "And take the flower child with you."

"Hey," said Toaster.

"Shut up," said Goff.

Swakely walked forward and stood in front of Goff with his hands on his hips. "Is that straight, Tarzan?"

Goff tipped the gun barrel upwards. "Move it."

"Sammy," called Swakely without turning his head. "Get Will and yourself into that wagon. Hurry it up."

Sammy ran to Kilbride and helped him to stand. He opened the front passenger door of the car and tried to ease Kilbride inside.

"Arthur," shouted Kilbride, both hands flat on the

roof. "Ask him if he's got a licence for that fucking cannon."

Sammy struggled with Kilbride, pressing on his head and pushing from behind. Kilbride fell into the car, striking his head on the door rim. Sammy lifted his legs and swung them towards the dashboard. "For fuck's sake," said Kilbride. "I'm in."

Sammy shut the passenger door and took a seat in the back of the car behind Kilbride. He looped his arm around Kilbride's shoulders and yelled through the window, "We're in, Arthur, we're in."

"Well," Swakely said to Goff, moving his shoulders. "If it's any consolation, I've never been so frightened in my life."

"Save the crap for the cabaret," said Goff.

"Yeah. Still," said Swakely. He raised his right hand to his shoulder, spreading his fingers. "Be lucky." He walked to the car and took the driving seat. He started the engine, dipping his head around Kilbride to nod at Goff, and moved in a low gear past the club and towards the exit. The front wheel left a damp trail of Kilbride's vomit.

"He recognized you," said Toaster.

"That's right," said Goff. "But he won't do anything about it."

"I just don't understand," said Toaster.

"I know you don't," said Goff, peeling off his mask. "You've got no respect for art."